GORE VIDAL wrote ... ...eteen
while overseas in World War II. ... Vidal
has written novels, plays, sh... ...en a
political activist. As a Democ... ...state
New York, he received the mo... ...ury.
...In
...lf-

... praised international bes... *he*
One of the television plays became the
w...ssful Broadway play *Visit to a Small Planet* (1957). Directly for the
...eater he wrote the prize-winning hit *The Best Man* (1960). In 1964
Vidal returned to the novel with *Julian*, the story of the apostate Roman
emperor. This novel has been published in many languages and
editions. As Henry de Montherlant wrote: "*Julian* is the only book about
a Roman emperor that I like to re-read. Vidal loves his protagonist; he
knows the period thoroughly; and the book is a beautiful hymn to the
twilight of paganism." During the last quarter-century Vidal has been
telling the history of the United States as experienced by one family
and its connections in what Gabriel García Márquez has called "Gore
Vidal's magnificent series of historical novels or novelized histories."
They are, in chronological order, *Burr, Lincoln, 1876, Empire, Hollywood,
Washington, D.C.* and *The Golden Age*.

During the same period, Vidal invented a series of satiric comedies –
Myra Breckinridge, Myron, Kalki, Duluth. "Vidal's development . . . along
that line from *Myra Breckinridge* to *Duluth* is crowned with success,"
wrote Italo Calvino in *La Repubblica* (Rome). "I consider Vidal to be a
master of that new form which is taking shape in world literature and
which we may call the hyper-novel or the novel elevated to the square
or to the cube." To this list Vidal added the highly praised – and
controversial – *Live from Golgotha* in 1992. *Palimpsest*, his highly
acclaimed memoir, was published in 1995 and was followed by *The
Smithsonian Institution*, published in 1998. The collection of his works –
The Essential Gore Vidal – was published in 1999.

Vidal has also published several volumes of essays. When the National
Book Critics Circle presented him with an award (1982), the citation
read: "The American tradition of independent and curious learning is
kept alive in the wit and great expressiveness of Gore Vidal's criticism."
In 1993, he won the National Book Award for *United States: Essays
1952–1992*.

Vidal co-starred with Tim Robbins in the movie *Bob Roberts*.

A THIRSTY EVIL

Gore Vidal

ABACUS

ABACUS

First published in Great Britain in 1956 by William Heinemann Ltd
Published in 1974 by Granada Publishing Limited in Panther Books
A print on demand book published by Abacus in 2005

A CIP catalogue record for this book
is available from the British Library.

ISBN 0 349 10656 8

Abacus
An imprint of
Time Warner Book Group UK
Brettenham House
Lancaster Place
London WC2E 7EN

www.twbg.co.uk

For
Howard Austen

Contents

Three Stratagems

I arrived in Key West a few days ago with enough money to last me a week. I seldom need more than a week, although this time I have gone more slowly than usual, with a greater attention to detail, ignoring the young, concentrating my attention on the older men, the ones with loose, dimpled figures and bad teeth. Watching these men, talking to them, I find it hard to believe that in other days they had made fortunes, created families and often as not done noble deeds, for with us they have neither shame nor virtue. Naturally it has occurred to me that they might be wise and still not care and then again there's the possibility that they enjoy their own degradation; if that's true, I pity them, and the game's more sinister than one might at first suppose.

The beach at Key West begins at the south end of the main street and continues for a hundred yards or so, edged by palm trees and beach houses and ending, finally, in a pink cement building, a restaurant with an outdoor terrace. On the beach, near this terrace, I met Mr. Royal my first day.

The sky was a startling, unclouded blue, and a warm south wind rattled the fronds of the palm trees. The day was brilliant, and for a moment I was sad and wanted to go and hide from the sun, from the white-framed image of the sea – associations all of childhood, of that contented season of sand forts and seaweed and pink shells. Every summer of my childhood was spent upon a similar beach with my family; a family which has since broken up: some dead, some married and others, myself among them, gone into exile in the foreign cities. . . .

'I see you haven't been here long.' His voice was pleasant, yet with a suggestion, oh, just the faintest suggestion, of something else. I was immediately alert. I told him I'd only just arrived, and he introduced himself. He told me he was George Royal, and he insisted too quickly that I call him George; so far I haven't. I told him my name was Michael.

'Could tell you haven't been here very long,' he continued, and we talked about the whiteness of my skin until at last he asked me if I'd ever been an athlete (that traditional question both wistful and vicious), and of course I said, yes. I told him I'd played football at Princeton, which was not true: I went to Princeton for one year, but I played no games; the lie impressed him, however. 'Let's have a drink,' he said.

Together we crossed the hot white beach, picking our way between gaudily-striped umbrellas, crumpled towels, bottles of lotion and empty beer-cans, all reminiscent once again of my childhood. Reminiscent and yet, in one particular, different: the people have changed; they have become hostile or at best they are dangerously impersonal. I realize, certainly, that perhaps *I* am so changed that I see them now as they really are, as they were all along . . . though of course it's always possible that what I first saw as a child was the reality and what I see now a private distortion, but one way or the other I see what I see: hostility and danger. I know that my attitude is extreme, that there are some innocuous people in the world and, more important, there are many fools and for *that* happy abundance at least I give thanks.

The fools were in possession of the beach today. They

sat watchfully beneath umbrellas, admiring the cold and radiant angels who could, they believed, exorcize the graceless shadows of the years and with firm flesh recreate youth and the sense of permanency, or its illusion. I suppose by now I know the hearts of the fools almost as well as I know my own, and sometimes I am frightened when I watch their sad courtship of the treacherous angels, for I see in them my own eventual fall from beloved angel to deluded monster. I too shall be old. I shuddered as I stepped over the ruined towers of a sand-castle: yes, the beach was changed; I wonder, will it change again one day?

In a mood of odd unreality, I followed the wide, sun-darkened figure of Mr. Royal to the cement terrace where, at tables, beneath umbrellas, men and women in bathing-suits sat in the vivid light and drank rum. In the bar, a juke-box played loudly and I am sure that no one heard what I could hear behind the music, the soft noise of the tide going out.

These people were well-to-do. Most of them were middle-aged and I thought that the men and women, except for the one obvious difference, looked exactly alike: wide hipped, sagging breasts, thin arms and legs, blue-veined and weak. But the women wore paint and moved with more assurance. They laughed, drank heavily, told dirty jokes, gambled and all in all endured the bright days gallantly. The men did not. They were quieter, more watchful; they were waiting.

Mr. Royal was looking at me expectantly. We had stopped walking and he had asked me a question which I'd not heard. Since we were standing beside an empty table, I made a guess, nodded and smiled and, having guessed correctly, we sat down. He ordered rum for both of us.

'I come down here every year,' said Mr. Royal, rubbing his small brown hands together: a yellow diamond glittered, a spray of bright sparks, of sunlight shattered. I looked away. He folded his hands and continued talking, looking over my shoulder at a party of sailors who had just arrived on the beach and were pulling off their clothes with shouts and giggles, like schoolgirls on an outing. I don't like sailors very much, not because they are, in a sense, competitors, but because their lack of direction, of a considered plan, their fundamental irresponsibility, tend to make them unsatisfactory playmates and, if taken seriously, they are often downright dangerous, in other words, they waste their beauty and their advantages.

I have often thought half-seriously that when I am old and *hors de combat*, I should like to start some sort of school for young men, a school where I would teach them how to make the most of certain situations which otherwise, due to inexperience and vanity, they badly mismanage. They are usually too truculent, too unbending. But then I suppose that if one of them had sense enough to come to me for lessons he'd be quite clever enough to conduct his own affairs without advice.

'The main business is in Newton but I have another store in Belmont,' said Mr. Royal, his eyes coming to focus on me again as he made this point.

'That sounds pretty interesting,' I said. At first one shouldn't talk too much, for talk reveals character and unless one is simple and artless and appealingly boyish, it's best not to talk at all, to remain silent and smiling, enigmatic, waiting for the proper moment to assume the character of the other's dream. It takes a good deal of experience and intuition to do this, for, to be successful, one must have some native power of divination to begin with, an ability to identify oneself correctly without engagement; it's not easy.

As Mr. Royal talked, I kept my eyes on the sea beyond him; I watched the solemn variations of gulls against blue and, as I did, I remembered that I'd seen no birds on this island and I wondered why there were none. Had they all been blown away by some hurricane? Or had there never been birds here? I watched the gulls and listened carefully, awaiting some sign, some omen. I have been cheated several times at the last minute, undergoing a singular martyrdom which, unlike the classic ones, persists without hope of relief and has, on more than one occasion, wrecked my plans. I have a feeling, however, that this time everything will go well; I've proceeded slowly and I am sure of Mr. Royal, if not of myself, for I suffer from the disease of visionaries without, sad to say, the compensating vision.

'I used to have a cottage here when Mrs. Royal was alive, but when she died I sold it and now I just take a few rooms at the Casa Rosada. You know it, don't you? Nice place. I like the manager, an old friend of mine.'

Three points: Mrs. Royal, her death, the rooms at the Casa Rosada . . . no, four points: the friendly manager. The fourth point gave meaning to the other three.

I looked at Mr. Royal. His eyes, I noticed, were dark and oriental-looking with black, shiny irises set in yellow whites and, about the irises, pale circles like rings of smoke indicated age.

'I walked by there this morning, on my way to the beach,' I said.

'But you haven't been inside?'

'No, like I said I only got here today.'

'That's right. You've only just arrived.'

'I haven't looked about yet.' I took a swallow of the

rum. The sun was hot and there was no wind. I was uncomfortable and I wished I was in the green water swimming, or back in my room. Mr. Royal asked me where I was staying. He nodded when I told him.

'A nice place,' he said, implying he knew a thing or two about nice places. 'But you really ought to stay at the Casa Rosada; that's the only place to stay in this town, the only place.'

I gestured and grinned, demonstrating without words that I could not afford an expensive hotel but that, even so, it made little difference to me, to one well-born. He was most tactful; he smiled shyly, showing a set of pretty white teeth with well-defined gums, pink and translucent; a fleck of tobacco on an incisor gave a certain authenticity to this cunning but rather formal craftsmanship.

Before we could speak further, more frankly, a man with long blond-silver hair came over to our table. 'Hello, George,' he said. His body was thin; through sun-burned skin the rib-cage showed, like an emaciated Christus carved with morbid detail in some Bavarian forest while, beneath the taut skin of his chest, pulled drum-tight over the bones, I could see the regular twitchings of his heart.

'Sit down, sit down,' said Mr. Royal. 'Haven't seen you anywhere today. How'd you make out last night? Here, meet my friend. He's a Princeton boy, just down from college, on vacation. He's a football player, too.' And so I was introduced to Joe.

'I did pretty well,' said Joe, glancing at me curiously. 'I'm tired today.' His face was so tanned I could not tell if he were young or not, sick or well.

'Joe here is a painter,' said Mr. Royal, drawing us together with a puppeteer's authority.

'I'm tired,' repeated Joe, blinking in the light. I noticed that his lips were trembling. 'Could I have a drink?' More rum was brought. I had now begun to sweat and felt better. I'd had no breakfast and the rum was having a familiar, a pleasant effect.

'I wanted to paint this morning,' said Joe.

'Why didn't you?' asked Mr. Royal, looking at the beach, his attention wandering: two boys were wrestling nearby. He blinked several times and then, before Joe could answer, he stood up vaguely and said: 'I'll be right back, got to make a phone call.'

'How long've you known him?' asked Joe, watching Mr. Royal's distracted progress across the terrace.

'I only got in town today. I met him today.'

White upon dark brown, his eyebrows curved. 'Good work,' said Joe, grinning. His face gleamed with sweat and his lips no longer trembled.

'What do you mean?'

'How do you like him?'

'I just met him. He seems all right.'

'One store is in Belmont and the other is in Newton.'

'Then you know everything. Have you met Hilda yet? No? Well, she is the other one. I got to get another drink. Be right back.'

'Yes, I know.'

Joe had been gone only a moment when Mr. Royal returned.

'Pleasant fellow, Joe, I like him . . . but then I like everybody. I never saw a man I didn't like,' said Mr. Royal.

'That's a good way to be.' I suppose during the last few years I've learned every neutral, every noncommittal remark there is.

'I think so. Life's too short, you know, and then there is a really swell group down here. You'll meet them all ... kind of free-living, of course, if you get what I mean. Anything goes ... that sort of thing. I hope you don't mind ... that sort of thing, I mean.'

'I don't mind anything,' I said, unfurling suddenly like a Jolly Roger, declaring bravely my own intended piracy in these rich waters. He was noticeably pleased, ready to be boarded and scuttled.

'You're so wise,' he exclaimed admiringly. 'Life's too · short not to enjoy every minute of it.' He paused. 'By the way, why don't you drop by the Casa Rosada this evening and have dinner with me? Might be fun and ...' His voice became an incoherent blur of cosy, ingenuous good fellowship.

'I think I can,' I said slowly. I looked up and saw Joe approaching us.

'Ah,' said Joe, sitting down. 'Wrestlers!' We all looked at the two young sailors wrestling on the beach, their white bodies streaked with red where the sand had burned them. 'Do you like to wrestle?' asked Joe, turning to me. I said no, and Mr. Royal, impervious to malice, repeated that I was a football player. 'I can see that,' said Joe, playing with two straws. He was going to say more when I asked Mr. Royal why there were no birds on this island, except for a few pelicans and the gulls out to sea.

II

I have always preferred the Casa Rosada to the other hotels in Florida, or anywhere, for that matter, simply because it's the best hotel in Key West and Key West remains my favourite place in all the world. I came here for the first time the winter before I was married. Until then I had always gone to Daytona Beach but, on the advice of a close friend, I came on down and I must say it was worth it. Fortunately, my wife liked it too, and until she died we spent every winter here. The island of course was much different in those days. There were fewer Cubans, for one thing, and the palm trees, as I remember, were straighter, unbent by hurricanes.

Shortly after the war, Mrs. Royal died in our house. I sold it immediately afterwards. I can't think, offhand, of a better place to die: a clear day with a south wind and the sun shining – what could be better? But of course she was in pain and that's always terrible. It must be a frightful sensation to know that one will not recover, that the pain will go on worsening until at last, like falling from some great height, one dies. I should live twenty more years, at least, barring accidents: touch wood. In any case if the fear should become unbearable I can always take up Christian Science or something like that. The worst thing of all, of course, is the realization that one will never be young again, like Michael. I can no longer remember what it was like to wake up in the morning without a burning sensation below my heart, without aching joints; although having all my teeth pulled did help the arthritis. I am sure he noticed them on the beach today. He looked rather closely at me once but then I imagine that everyone sees they are false. I suppose I'll get used to them in time.

While I dressed that first night I wondered if he would be on time, if he would come at all. My hands trembled as I tied my tie, a dark red one, very discreet, not loud at all, for I knew, instinctively, that he was special, not like the rest of the trade around here. I also made up my mind not to be too hearty. With him I would be subdued but responsive, moving slowly and with careful gestures, rather as though I were dealing with a strange dog, the kind that doesn't bark. We all have, I suppose, a certain ideal, a ghost we've dreamed of but never met. From the beginning Michael corresponded to that inner dream of mine.

As I went down in the elevator at five-thirty, half an hour early (there was just a chance he might already have arrived and gone to the bar), I reminded myself that I was, after all, a man of the world and that there was no reason to be too impressed by this young man. But I was. I could not help it.

I have always enjoyed the terrace of the Casa Rosada. The view of the sea beyond the palms is first-rate in the early evening. Behind me the lights of the hotel were being turned on and white-coated waiters moved up and down the brick terrace, attending to the guests who sat about, drinking quietly. And there it was above the palms like a bead of silver: star bright star light, first star I've seen tonight . . . oh, the same thing, the same wish, always the same thing.

'Shall I bring you something, sir?'

'Yes, a martini. I'll have it here.' I sat down at a table. Michael had not arrived yet: I could see the bar through an open french window and there was no one there. Everyone was outside in the cool air. I was wondering if perhaps he'd left a message for me at the desk when I was diverted by the arrival of Joe and Hilda.

'Hi, George, I'm dog-tired. Do you mind if we sit down? I've been all over town with Joe, pub-crawling. We can't do things like that at our age, can we?'

Hilda is sixty-five. At thirty-five she became a widow

and at thirty-seven she made a fortune on Wall Street; as far as I know she still has every penny she ever made, for she seldom picks up a check except of course when she is with one of her court of extremely sissy young men; they are transients for the most part and so much alike they seem interchangeable. Joe has been a figure at court for some time now.

While Hilda talked of her day I gave orders to the waiter, smiled at Joe and looked at my watch: it was five forty-five. Fifteen minutes to go. I concentrated on Hilda. She wore bright colours tonight, yellow and green, and her hard dark face glowed. She looked like one of the more bitter of the Old Testament prophets. I have known her for twenty years and, until my wife died, we were most discreet with one another; since then, however, we've let our hair down, as the saying goes, and the hairpins flew in all directions when we did. As I suspected, she had known everything for some time and I, certainly, had always known of her own activities, for, by a not unusual though sad coincidence, our interests often overlapped and we were, and are, more rivals than friends, more enemies than allies. Nevertheless, I feel a kind of affection for her. We have survived the same wars and we have known the same years and when we look at one another we alone can see the true face behind the wrinkles, the firm line of the jaw beneath loose skin.

'And Joe thinks he's terribly attractive. What's his name?'

Whose name? Five minutes to six. 'Michael. He's from Princeton.'

'Watch out! There's always something wrong when they pull that college business. It means they're out for big game.'

'And you think I'm in season?'

'Yes and I see you mounted right now.' They roared with laughter while I smiled, not bothering to defend him. Why should I? Hilda always suspects the worst of everyone and, though she's seldom disappointed, I must say I think she's wrong about *him*: he is different ... whether for good or bad, however, I'm not able to determine, even now. I look for the best in everyone, myself, and on the surface he is dignified, apparently well-educated and he has been around. He has no money, which is always fortunate for me; it's no worse to be loved for one's money than to be loved for something as spurious and impermanent as beauty. One must be practical and the thing to bear in mind, I've found, is not *why* one receives certain attentions but the attentions themselves. There are, of course, times when it is a most desperate business to realize one's only attraction is solvency, never to experience that tenuous response, that identification which, if all goes well, becomes love, or so they say. I wouldn't know, although for a minute or two at a time in my youth I knew what it must be like. Ah, Michael. It was six o'clock.

'Are you waiting for someone, George? You keep looking at your watch.'

I nodded and Joe smirked unpleasantly; fortunately, I was not asked to elaborate, for Hilda had begun a familiar chant. 'All morning I walked along the beach among the beauties,' she intoned in her resonant strong voice, a voice more suited for denunciation than for idle talk. 'And I found I loved them all. Isn't that tragic? It gives me such a pang when I remember that I am over fifty and that there's no time for them all!' She chuckled darkly, Jeremiah among the cacti. 'But I get along, don't I, Joe? I do my best.'

'I'll say,' said Joe admiringly and I wondered, as I often have before, why they are always drawn to this sort of woman: did such a woman take the shears to them in their youth?

'Today I watched one dressing on the highway, behind some rocks. Joe and I were bicycling and we'd stopped for a second where the road bends, just beyond where the boats are. I've never seen such beauty, never! I wanted to weep.'

'Or do something else?' I suggested mildly. Hilda is always too vehement and her stories embarrass me for they are all like this one, *voyeur* stories. She shook her head, however: the goddess with the shears triumphant – or, perhaps, a sickle would be more in keeping, more Greek.

'No, not that,' said Hilda rather sharply. 'I didn't feel like that at all.'

' "There was a boy; ye know him well, ye cliffs and island of Winander?" '

'Is that a poem?' asked Hilda.

'Yes, that's a poem,' said Joe. 'Look, George, there he is, the boy himself.'

'Is he like the boy in the poem?' asked Hilda, squinting near-sightedly.

'No, dear, the boy in the poem died at twelve. Come, let's go. Maybe, we'll see you later.'

I nodded. 'Yes, of course, later.' Joe led the reluctant Hilda away before Michael arrived.

'I hope I'm not late.'

'No, you're right on time. Would you like a little something?' A little something was brought us.

'You look flushed tonight.'

'I was burned a bit: too much sun for the first day.'

We talked about the beach, the day, the latitude, the

weather and the cause of storms. I noticed again how well-bred he looked. He wore a tweed jacket and slacks and a dark knit tie; I was glad I hadn't worn an open shirt – so far all my intuitions had been correct – and, finally, when I told him that dinner had been set up in my suite, he was not surprised; he remarked it was nice to dine quietly.

My living-room is quite large, on a corner, with tall windows and a view of the hotel gardens and the sea.

'It's lovely on a moonlit night,' I said, indicating the dark gardens and the darker sea, vague by starlight.

Then I lit the candles on the table and turned out the overhead light. One gets rather like a vain woman as one grows older: morbidly aware of lighting, of the clash of colours, of shadows and unbecoming angles. A great actress once told me that the best light for an ageing woman was a full direct one which made no shadow. To benefit from that sort of lighting, however, the bone structure must be very good; if it's not, too much light is disastrous. I'm afraid *I* must do with candlelight. And, 'bone structure' always makes me think of a grinning skull.

During dinner we discussed, among other things, that what the Floridians call lobsters aren't lobsters at all.

'I remember taking a trip in a sailboat up to Maine, to a place called Camden, where we lived on lobster mostly. We used to broil them on the beach, with seaweed and driftwood.' He talked freely, his first wariness gone. In some detail he told me about his life. And as I listened I was, as usual, perplexed, for my first impulse is to believe everything I am told and my first reaction is to believe nothing; consequently, I am doomed for ever to dangle between belief and doubt.

His father was a lawyer in Washington. His father is

dead. Graduating from Princeton four years ago, Michael went to Europe and took a job with American Express. He quit his job and came home; he has no job now. He wants to travel. He is engaged to be married. As I listened, I drank wine and, after a while, I became a little confused and I was forced, now and then, to ask him to repeat himself, to clarify certain obscurities. Yet all the time while he was telling me he was to be married, I recognized response and, bold with wine, I discussed his love with him, hovering closer and closer to that revelation which, with an inner trembling, I hardly dared anticipate. 'She's only nineteen, but when she finishes college next year we're going to be married. Naturally there's the problem of money but I'm sure something will turn up by then; I mean it always does. Her father's one of the biggest attorneys in Washington so I'm pretty sure he can fix me up. I think I might like to go into the Foreign Service one day.'

'I'm sure you'd be very good at it.' As he talked, I noticed his face was scarlet and his eyes were brilliant in the uneven light of the candles; then, suddenly watching him, I realized that here before me was the beloved figure materialized, no longer a figure to haunt the night or an elusive expression remarked for a moment in a stranger's face, a similarity, which, upon examination, would vanish, like a gold doubloon found on a beach in a dream and gone upon awakening, the sensation of it clutched tightly in one's palm lingering to mock the day. I knew, as I watched him, that all of the others had been, at best, facsimiles: although, of course, I received them, for I am realistic, I think, and I had never actually hoped to encounter my ghost except in that feverish period between waking and sleeping when degrading and marvellous visions compensated me for the days of nothing, for the days of approximation. Fascinated, I watched him across the table.

III

Now, since that night with Michael, I have learned a lot about epilepsy. It seems that Julius Caesar and Mohammed, among other celebrities, were epileptics and until quite recently there wasn't much to be done about their malady. According to a medical encyclopaedia I found in the manager's office, it has something to do with an overcharge of nervous electricity in the body, a bit like a short circuit, I suppose. Each case varies, of course, although there are only two main types: the 'grand sickness' and the 'little sickness'. The 'little' isn't particularly bothersome; one drifts off for a second or two and that's that. The 'grand', however, is more serious and very frightening to watch, as I found out.

At first I thought he'd had a stroke. A great many of my contemporaries are dying of strokes these days, and whenever anyone faints or is sick my impulse is to call a doctor who will, if it's not too late, inject adrenalin. But then I realized that he was too young to have a stroke, and for one insane moment I thought that he was putting on a show for me. I stood over him, helpless, wondering what to do, but then, when he began to choke, I called the house physician, for the boy sounded as if he were strangling to death which, by the way, could very easily have happened, for epileptics have been known to swallow their tongues and die.

The doctor, thank heavens, was very calm and he gave me a spoon to hold Michael's tongue in place while he administered a shot of some sort. In a moment the convulsions stopped and he lay quietly on the floor among the broken dishes (the table had turned over in the confusion). After a minute or two, the doctor got him to his feet. 'I'll put him up for the night downstairs,' he said. 'I expect he'll be all right now.' I helped the doctor with him as far as the elevator. Michael was conscious by now, but too exhausted to speak intelligibly.

So, for the time at least, the ghost is vanished, obscured and distorted by that figure among the shattered dishes upon the floor. I haven't talked to him since, although I did see him earlier today on the beach. We did not speak. He was with an old friend of mine, a man named Jim Howard. Jim is a grand fellow about my age or, perhaps, a little older. At one time he was very wealthy, but he hasn't a dime now. They seem to be getting on very well, however, and it will be interesting to see what happens.

1950

The Robin

At nine I was very much tougher than I am now. I enjoyed all sorts of unpleasant things: other people's fights (I was early an audience), automobile accidents, stories of suicides and one particular peep-show at an amusement park near Washington where, through holes in a tall imitation stockade, one could observe an immense plaster elephant goring a plaster Hindu. But best of all I liked the magazines sold in drugstores, magazines with pictures of young women entangled in giant spider webs on their covers, and inside, pictures of the most exciting scenes of torture. I used to sit for hours on the tile floor of a certain drugstore and carefully examine all the magazines. Sometimes I even read the stories. I liked very much the directness, the naturalness of the style. I had long since become bored with the colourless fourth-grade reader and I hadn't yet discovered the Oz books which, at ten, helped bring to an end my tough period.

In the fourth grade I had one close friend: a thin, pale-haired, pale-eyed, pale-skinned boy whose name was Oliver. I suppose he has since grown up to become a lawyer or a realtor. Most boys from our group in Washington become either one or the other. To my knowledge none has become anything interesting like a movie star or an artist, though a number have been divorced once or twice and several show signs of alcoholism.

Oliver loved violence and torture as much as I did, and he was almost as tough as I was, and that was very tough indeed. Our conversation was a mixture of gangster and nursery talk. We organized secret societies, encouraged gang warfare at school, and sometimes we even went to grocery stores and stole.

All of us had elaborate dream worlds. I can guess now what Oliver's was probably like; as for my own, I can remember it vividly: the climate, the scenery and even various plots of my imaginary life when I was nine and depraved. I know that I had great physical strength and lived in a castle, wore a cloak and very often a crown. I was not only stronger than the other nine-year-olds, I was stronger than grown men too: that deep-voiced, rough-faced alien race. And in my world I invented all sorts of tortures for my enemies. The most constant and satisfactory victim was the fourth-grade teacher, a shapeless woman with bobbed hair, grey and untidy, and a dreadful nose that was thin with a pink, translucent membrane. She almost always had a cold and a fever blister on her upper lip. She was stern, malicious and, in moments of anger, an arm-twister. She received her reward in *my* world.

About the middle of October, shortly after my ninth birthday, on a clear bright afternoon, Oliver and I saw the robin.

First, let me say that our school was what they call a country day school, several miles from the city. The school had broad, well-kept lawns where less imaginative boys resolved their violence in football and fighting. Oliver and I seldom joined them; we were contemptuous of such simplicity. Sometimes of course we were forced to play, and when that happened I'd pick a part of the field where nothing much was going on to disturb me, and here I would stand and day-dream. In these dreams I was the actor, never the audience.

The school occupied a large country home in Virginia some ten minutes by bus from Washington. The house was what we, in that part of the South, call Georgian, though actually it was a gracious late nineteenth-century muddle of styles: red-brick, with tall windows on the ground floor and, inside, a curving staircase. There were high ceilings, cracks in the walls, and everywhere the sense of many generations of Southern feudal life; actually, the house was the relic of a rich Northerner who, having come south with a Republican administration, built this house, fancied himself a squire, willed it to his children, died, and they, true heirs, promptly sold it.

But to us, the sixty pupils, the grounds were far more interesting than the house: smooth lawns curved from the house to the line of woods where, between thin dark trees bright in autumn with the colours of the fall, one could just make out the brown slow Potomac River which roared continuously, sea-like and far away, a sad, lonely sound.

The day of the robin was like any other day of autumn. I caught the school bus in front of my house and talked to Oliver as we drove to school. I haven't the faintest idea what our conversations were like when we were nine.

I suppose that Oliver and I discussed our teachers, the other boys and the peculiarities of our parents. I do remember once turning to him and saying solemnly (this was a year later, after my mother's divorce): 'We've gone through hell and high water together, my mother and I.' By the time I was ten I do recall that I talked almost entirely in sonorous clichés and I had begun to demonstrate an alarming talent for moral poetry. But at nine, on this sharp October day, I was more colourful, more desperate and certainly more original than I've ever been since.

We arrived at the school, entered the class-room, and here recollection ceases. I suppose something must have happened in those classes, but I cannot remember what. During the twelve years I spent in schools, I remember almost nothing that happened in the class-rooms. I have only one clear memory of my first six years in school. For some reason we built a model of the Appian Way on a card-table. And since, among my numerous talents, I had a gift for modelling, I was invited to make the human figures for the Appian Way. They were beautiful, splendid Romans, happily proportioned, clothed in togas of the whitest tissue paper. Everyone was impressed. But unfortunately they would not stand up and the teacher, that thin-lipped terrible woman, squashed all the legs down to fat columns, completely ruining their classic symmetry. When I discovered this, I gave such a demonstration of outraged sensibility that she was forced to call in the principal, who tried to soothe me by suggesting that with longer togas no one would notice the legs, and, besides I should remember I had been commissioned to do figures (very admirable they were, too) which could stand up in chariots.

Apart from this one episode I remember nothing of those six years in the class-room, but I do remember the afternoons out of doors, especially this particular afternoon in October. The sky was pale and the clouds were heavy and white and they moved so slowly, changed shape so slowly that one was quite hypnotized watching the castles become elephants, and the elephants swans, and the swans teachers. On this day Oliver and I unobtrusively slipped away from our game-playing classmates.

We walked quickly to the edge of the lawn where a wooded cliff dropped nearly vertical to the river below.

Here, hidden from the others by a row of evergreens, the river beneath us, we sat comfortably on the ground and I began to make up a story while Oliver listened eagerly, flatteringly.

It was he who noticed the robin first. 'Look,' he said, interrupting me, pointing at something in the grass. I looked and saw the bird. One of its wings had been broken and it fluttered feebly, still trying to fly. We went over and examined it carefully, but wary of touching it for fear of an unexpected sting or bite or sinister germs.

'What'll we do?' I asked. One always had to do something about everything that came one's way.

Oliver shook his head; he was no use. 'It's hurt bad.' We watched the robin as it fluttered in a small circle on the ground. It made a small piping sound.

'Maybe we ought to take it home.' But Oliver shook his head: 'It's hurt too bad. It's not going to live long and, anyway, we wouldn't know what to do.'

'Maybe we should get some witch hazel or something,' I suggested; but since this meant approaching the authorities of the school, we decided against doctoring.

I have forgotten whose idea it was first. I hope it was Oliver's. We decided the robin must be put out of its misery; it must be killed. The decision was made easily enough, but when it came to the actual execution we were not only uninventive but frightened.

Thinking of a picture I had seen of Saint Stephen, I suggested the robin be killed with a stone. Oliver took the first stone (I'm almost certain it was Oliver) and dropped it directly on top of the creature, but the stone fell to one side and the bird, still alive, fluttered its wings and gasped. Then *I* took a stone and dropped it and now, horribly, there was blood on the wings that fluttered in the bright air, that fanned the dead leaves on the ground.

Then we grew frightened and angry and we took more stones and threw them as hard as we could at the robin, anything to stop the motion of those wings and the sound of pain. The stones fell one upon another until the bird was covered except for its head . . . and still it was not dead: it would not die. Oliver (I am sure now it was Oliver) finally took a very large stone and smashed it as hard as he could on top of the pyramid, finishing the tomb. Then we listened carefully: there were no more sounds from within.

We stood for a long time, not looking at one another, the pile of stones between us. No sound but the distant shouts of our classmates playing on the lawn. The sun shone brilliantly; nothing had changed in the world, but suddenly, without a word and at the same moment, we both began to cry.

1948

A Moment of Green Laurel

My absent-mindedness seems to have only to do with places; I have little difficulty in recalling either names or faces and I usually get to appointments on time although, even in this, I've become a bit careless lately.

Last week I arrived for an appointment not only at the wrong hour but at the wrong address, a somewhat disturbing experience. But now the Treasury Building was straight ahead and I was relieved that I could still find my way so easily through the streets of Washington, a city I'd not lived in for many years.

Thousands of people crowded the pavements, for this was Inauguration Day and all were eager to watch the new President ride in state to the Capitol for the Inaugural ceremony. The crowd was in gala mood though the sky was dull, promising rain.

With difficulty, I crossed the street to Willard's Hotel. At the kerb I was stopped by the pillar of some mid-Western community, a pillar now wreathed in alcohol. In one hand he carried a small banner and in the other a bottle of whisky with no label (I did not then guess the significance of this detail). 'Things going to change in this town. Take it from me.' Gracefully, I took it from him and, avoiding the bottle proffered, moved as quickly as I could to the hotel entrance, and went inside.

Willard's has two lobbies: one on the 'F' street side and one on the Pennsylvania Avenue side, parallel to it; the lobbies are connected by a carpeted, mirrored, marbled corridor where I was able to find a sofa to sit on that I might comfortably observe the hundreds of people who now passed from street to avenue, all hurry-ing, all delighted.

Out of loyalty to our elegant Washington society, I decided these noisy passers-by must be from out of town: thick business-men with rimless glasses, South-Westerners with stetsons and boots, New York ladies in silver fox – all political and all, for one reason or another, well-pleased with the new President. Some car-ried whisky-flasks, I noticed: the first I'd seen since I was a child and Prohibition was, in theory, law. Now, appar-ently, flasks had come back, as the advertisers would say.

A political personage sat down beside me, his right buttock, a bony one, glancing off my thigh as he squeezed a place for himself on the sofa. He wiggled about, making more room for himself. I scowled, un-noticed.

'You sure get mighty tired standing around,' he said at large, stumbling on truth. I agreed. He was Southern and he talked to me and from time to time I nodded with discreet half-attention, pretending to look for someone, hoping to excuse thereby my inattention. I even squinted near-sightedly as though a familiar face had suddenly appeared among strangers. Then one did. I saw my grandfather, white-haired and ruddy-faced, ap-proach with a political colleague. He was smiling at something the other was saying. As they passed in front of me, I heard my grandfather say: 'He knows as well as you do what I think of gold . . .'

By the time I'd got to my feet, upsetting the South-erner, the ghost was gone. My stomach contracted ner-vously; it had been someone else, of course. I have always had a habit of looking for likenesses. I will often notice a young boy and think: 'Why, there's so-and-so!

He was in school with me.' Then I'd recall that my acquaintance would be a grown man by now, no longer fourteen. Nevertheless, disturbed by this vision of my dead grandfather, I got to my feet and went into the Pennsylvania Avenue lobby. Here, among palms and portraits of the new President, more politicians and hangers-on celebrated the great moment with noise, whisky and thunderous good will.

'Come on up,' said a woman beside me. She was blonde, well-dressed, a little drunk and in a friendly mood. 'We've got a suite upstairs. We're having a party. We're going to watch the parade. ... Emily!' And Emily joined us too and we all went up in the elevator together.

The suite was two rooms hired weeks in advance for this day. The party had already begun: thirty or forty men and women, young office-holders for the most part, although there were, I soon discovered, some native Washingtonians too: parasitic figures to the business of government.

I was given a glass of champagne and left alone. My hostess and Emily, arm in arm, broke through circle after circle, penetrating to the centre of the party. I could hear their laughter long after they had vanished.

I moved slowly about the room. It was like a dance and I wished for the sake of appearance that I had a partner. There is something profoundly negative about standing alone on the outskirts of a group where everyone has arrived, like animals in a Noah's Ark, in twos, and departs in twos. I thought of floods.

I finished the champagne, wondering idly why I knew no one in the room. 'The city's changed,' I thought; I'd been away ten years, a long time. I crossed the room to the window and looked out at the parade which had begun. Loud-speakers at each street corner made the Inaugural Address audible but unintelligible. Something had gone wrong with the synchronization, and the loud-speakers echoed one another dismally, confusing the Presidential voice. The woman next to me remarked: 'It doesn't make any sense.'

I looked at her and saw to my surprise that it was my mother who had spoken. 'What're you doing here?' I asked.

'What am I . . .?' She looked puzzled. 'Dorothy – you know Dorothy, don't you? – asked . . .' There was too much noise and I didn't hear the rest of the sentence.

'But I thought you were going to stay home today?' She looked at me oddly and I realized she hadn't heard me. Conversation was now impossible. People shoved us, gave us drinks, greeted her enthusiastically. As I watched her I wondered, as I often do, at all the people she knows. It was apparent that during the many years I have been away from Washington, a whole new group had come to town and she knew them all.

'How long've you been here?' she asked brightly.

'I got here just a few minutes ago.'

'No, I meant how long . . .' But a large cavalry officer came between us. Isolated by his enormous, uniformed back, I looked out the window.

The sky was pale. Night loitered behind the dome of the Capitol where the President, with unusual resonance for him, had just finished his address. Below my window, soldiers were marching and the mob which lined both sides of the Avenue murmured at their ordered progress.

'How do you like it?' my mother asked, pitching her voice above the noise of the room; the cavalry officer had gone.

'Just like all the others we've seen.'

'I meant Washington.'

I paused. We had been through this so many times before. 'Well, you know what I think. . . .'

'I know . . .?'

'I meant it's just as dull as it always was.' Then I thought she said: 'How long did you live here before?' But since there was now so much confusion in the room I was not positive. I cleared my throat; men separated us. She was looking, I thought, extremely handsome. I hadn't seen her look so fine in years.

But now something unusual was happening outside. The noise of the crowd increased its volume like a radio being turned up or like an approaching earthquake which, in earthquake countries, can always be heard minutes in advance: a distant rumbling as the ground ripples in ever-widening circles from the disturbed centre. Responding to this urgent sound, the people in the room pushed against the windows and looked out just as the President passed beneath us in an open car. He lifted his top hat and waved it. Then he was gone and the shouting died away.

'Are you going back to the house?' I asked, turning to my mother. We were together again, circled by Air Corps officers.

She frowned vaguely. 'I suppose I'll see you later . . . some time,' she added and, before I could answer, a squad of women, wearing paper hats and blowing horns, divided the room with the fury of their passage and I took that wise moment to leave the party, narrowly avoiding the gift of a paper hat.

I wondered, as I walked back to the hotel, why my mother had been at that party. I realize that she knows a good many people nowadays that I don't know: people who've come to town in the years I have been away, travelling farther and farther from Washington, without regret or longing, always conscious, however, that nostalgia for place may yet occur in time. My family is a sentimental one and more and more I tend to believe in the heredity of behaviour. I shall probably be very moved one day at the thought of spring (or autumn) in Rock Creek Park where most of my childhood was spent, in a grey stone house on a hill, bordered by a steep lawn, by maple and oak trees, among hills evenly crossed by the rock-littered, ironbrown Rock Creek whose bright course winds through those green woods.

As I walked, I contemplated the election and the Inauguration which meant much less to me than I publicly pretended. I have a conviction that individuals have little to do with state affairs, that governments are essentially filing systems which in time break down for lack of cabinet space, clerks, typewriters, paper and perhaps, faith in order. More and more I find it difficult to take public matters seriously: a definite schizoid tendency, as a psychologist friend of mine would say, placing me figuratively in a grey rubber sack where, cut off from the world outside, I might regard with neither pleasure nor dismay the interior of my private realm, complacent at having escaped so neatly, so thoroughly.

I was now on the outskirts of Rock Creek Park. Obeying an impulse, I turned into the Park and walked down to Broad Branch Road, past Pierce's Mill – named for that good President who gave Hawthorne a consulate.

As I walked, day ended. The planet Venus, a circle of silver in a green sky, pierced the edge of the evening while the wintry woods darkened about me and in the stillness the regular sound of my footsteps striking the pavement was like the rhythmic beating of a giant stone heart.

At last I came to the hill where, at the top of a serpentine drive, our old house stood, a solid grey house, owned now by strangers. I was about to continue on, when a young boy crossed the road, coming from the creek.

He was half-grown with silver-blond hair and dark eyes. In his arms he carried several branches of laurel, When he saw me, he stopped. Then, magically, the street lamps went on, ending twilight, shadowing our faces.

'You live up there?'

'Yes.' His voice was light, not yet changed. He moved the green branches from one arm to another, tentatively, as though undecided whether to stay and talk or go home. 'It's my grandfather's house.'

'Have you lived there long?'

'Most of my life. You know my grandfather?'

I said I did not. 'But I used to live in that house, too ₅ ₅ . when I was about your age. *My* grandfather built it thirty years ago.'

'No, I don't think so. *Mine* built it a long time ago: when I was born.'

I smiled, not questioning this. 'How old are you?' I asked.

'Twelve,' he said, embarrassed he was not older. In the unshaded white light, his hair glittered like metal.

Then I asked the traditional questions about school: adults and children meet always as foreigners with a limited common vocabulary and mutual distrust. I should have liked to talk to him as an equal, I thought: my eyes on the green only, not on silver or on brown skin. There was a directness about him which is rare among children, who usually are not only careful but often downright political in their dealings with the larger people. I asked questions by rote: 'What do you like best in school?'

'Reading. My grandfather has a big library . . .'

'In the attic,' I said, remembering my own childhood.

'Yes, in the attic,' he said, wonderingly. 'How did you know?'

'We kept books there, too, thousands of them.'

'So do we. I like the history ones.'

'And the *Arabian Nights*.'

He looked surprised. 'Yes. How did you know?'

I nodded, looking at him directly for the first time: a square brown face between silver hair and green laurel, a beardless, smooth face, uncomplicated by lines or dry skin or broken veins or by character which, once formed, like a poison in the blood, corrupts the face. The street lamp was directly overhead revealing the familiar skull. We looked at one another and I knew I should say something, ask yet another question, but I could not and so we stood until at last, to stop this silence, I repeated: 'Do you like school?'

'No. You live in Washington?'

'I used to . . . when I lived up there.' I indicated the hill. 'Before the war.'

'That was a long time ago,' said the boy frowning, and time, I remembered, depends on how old one is: ten years, nothing to me now, was all his life.

'Yes, a long time ago.'

He shifted his weight from one foot to another. 'Where do you live?'

'In New York . . . sometimes. Have you been there?'

'Oh, yes. I don't like it.'

I smiled, remembering as a child the prejudice Washington people had for New York. 'What are you going to do with these?' I asked, touching a branch of laurel. 'Make wreaths the way the Romans did?' I remembered an illustrated Victorian edition of Livy in which all the heroes wore Apollo's laurel.

He looked at me with surprise; then he smiled. 'Yes, I do that sometimes.'

'Nothing has changed,' I thought, and the terror began.

'I have to go,' he said, stepping out of the circle of light.

'Yes, it's time for dinner.'

From the top of the hill a woman's voice called a name which made us both start.

'I have to go,' he said again. 'Good-bye.'

'Good-bye.'

I watched him as he clambered straight up the hill and across the lawn, not following the paved driveway. I continued to watch until the front door opened and he stepped into the yellow light. Then, as I walked away, down the road between the dark evening hills, I wondered if I should ever recall an old encounter with a stranger who had asked me odd questions about our house, and about the green laurel which I carried in my arms.

1949

The Zenner Trophy

I

'I understand that Sawyer left early this morning, before anyone had a chance to talk to him, before the faculty met.' The Principal was appropriately grave.

'That's correct, sir,' said Mr. Beckman. 'And according to his adviser he left most of his clothes behind,' he added, as though by a very close examination of all detail he might somehow avoid the crisis. He had been at the School less than a year and although he'd faced any number of trying situations at other schools, he was by no means prepared to handle a disaster as vast as this one.

Fortunately, the Principal was a rock. In twenty years he had become the School or rather the School had been reshaped in his own image, to the delight of everyone except the faculty old guard. When he spoke he was able to do so with total knowledge and total authority; not only could he quote the entire constitution of this century-old academy but he could also make cogent analogies between today and yesterday, this century and the last. Rather like an Arab sage, thought Mr. Beckman, as the Principal made a precise and intelligent comparison between the present crisis and an earlier one, for, like the Arab philosophers, he assembled the main facts and then produced – from memory not from reason – a relevant antique text which gave him his solution, shaped by precedent and the cumulative wisdom of an old institution.

'Such an efficient man,' thought Mr. Beckman

nodding intelligently, not listening, too much absorbed by his sincere appreciation of this splendid human being who had saved him the year before from Saint Timothy's where he'd been an underpaid history instructor with nothing to look forward to but a future of dim discomfort, of dining-hall dinners (cold tuna fish, brown lettuce, potato chips and canned peas) made edible only by the frequent, the ritualistic use of a richly carved pepper-mill given him by the parents of a subnormal pupil he had befriended. But the previous spring his luck had changed; he was offered a summer job of tutoring a boy at Oyster Bay. He had accepted the assignment, enjoyed the summer and the company of the boy's uncle who, by a fortunate coincidence, was the Principal himself. ... 'And here I am,' thought Mr. Beckman complacently, crossing his legs and leaning forward, tuning in again, as it were, on his chief.

'And so, Mr. Beckman, you can see that this distasteful business is not by any means unfamiliar. We have faced it squarely in the past and no doubt we will have to face it again in the future, as squarely, alas.' He paused, allowing that classical epithet of sorrow, that stylized expression of grief to represent his attitude towards not only this particular instance of viciousness but towards all moral lapses, in school and out.

'I see what you mean, sir. Even at Saint Timothy's there was a similar case ...'

'I know, Mr. Beckman, I know,' interrupted the Principal. 'It is the spectre of all schools and the ruin of some; but not ours, Mr. Beckman, not ours.' The Principal smiled proudly up at the portrait of himself over the mock fireplace. It was a good portrait, painted in the Sargent manner, idealized but recognizable. The Principal gazed at his own portrait, as though drawing strength from this official version of himself, strength from the confident knowledge that this work would hang for generations in the chapel of the School, a decorative symbol of the reign of the thirteenth Principal, a likeness which would impress everyone with the distinguished arrangement of the features: a large, strong nose, a firm, lipless mouth, white brows and a full head of hair. In every respect it was the face of a man of power (that the body was small and fat made no difference, for it was hidden by academic robes). Then, sustained by this vision of his own posterity, the Principal returned to his vexing problem or, as it soon developed, Mr. Beckman's vexing problem.

'You have seen, sir, the speed with which the School has acted.' Mr. Beckman nodded, wondering if anyone since Dr. Johnson had so achieved the knack of making the ordinarily respectful 'sir' sound a cosy diminutive. 'We have always moved quickly in these matters. The ... revelation was made last night. By ten o'clock this morning the faculty, a majority of the faculty at least, had met and acted. That's quick action. Even *you* must admit that.'

Mr. Beckman admitted that it was very quick indeed: the 'even you' was the Principal's little joke, for he liked to pretend that Mr. Beckman was a critical and supercilious outsider, a spy from the Church academies, eager to find fault with this sternly Protestant school.

'Now Sawyer, it seems, has preferred to leave before his fate was made known to him. A cowardly flight but on the whole sensible, for there would have been no doubt in his mind as to what our decision would be: by leaving, he has saved us a certain embarrassment. I've written to his parents already.' He paused as though expecting some words of approbation from Mr. Beckman;

none came, for Mr. Beckman was now studying the portrait and wondering to himself what future generations would say when they saw it in the chapel: 'Who was that ape?' The irreverent thought amused him and he faced the original of the painting with a smile which the Principal interpreted as applause. Nodding abruptly as though both to acknowledge and silence a cheering crowd, the Principal continued. 'I believe I have presented the case quite dispassionately. I feel that the facts speak for themselves, as facts will, and that it would be gratuitous of me to make further comment. The responsibility is no longer mine but theirs. *Sawyer is no longer one of us.* Flynn, however, presents a more difficult problem.'

'You mean because he *hasn't* left?'

The Principal shook his head and he looked, thought Mr. Beckman, somewhat anxious. 'No, although I must say it might have helped matters if he'd gone when the other did. But that's not the trouble.'

'The Trophy?'

'Exactly. The Carl F. Zenner Award for clean sportsmanship, our highest honour. He was, if you remember, an extremely popular choice.'

'I certainly do remember. The boys cheered him for hours in chapel. I thought they'd never stop.'

The Principal nodded glumly. 'Fortunately the Trophy itself is not presented until Commencement Day; we have at least a week in which to consider what's to be done. Flynn of course can't have it now. I must say I wish we hadn't made the announcement so far in advance, but it's done and that's that and we'll have to make the best of it. I favour re-awarding it, but the Athletics Director tells me Flynn was the only possible choice – our finest athlete.' He paused. 'Do you remember the day he pitched against Exeter? Marvellous! Quite a good-looking boy, too. But I'm afraid I never knew him well.' The Principal was, in every way, the modern head of a great school: aloof, majestic, concerned only with the more abstract theories of education as well as the unrelenting. Grail-like quest for endowments. He had met very few of his youthful charges. In any case after thirty years, one boy tends to be very like another.

'Yes, he was a fine athlete,' agreed Mr. Beckman and he wondered how he might extricate his chief from this dilemma. The problem was partly his, since the boy had been his advisee. Each boy had an official adviser among the faculty. The duties of these advisers, however, were somewhat ill-defined; they were generally thought to be responsible for the academic careers of their advisees, but actually they were policemen, commissioned to keep order in the dormitories. The boy, Flynn, had been one of Mr. Beckman's charges and until now he had been his dormitory's chief ornament; he was the best athlete the School had produced in over a decade; so celebrated was he, in fact, that Mr. Beckman had been somewhat shy with him and consequently had not come to know him well.

'We must keep this from the students,' said the Principal suddenly, looking at Mr. Beckman as though he suspected him of giddiness, of tale-bearing.

'I quite agree, sir, but I'm afraid that they'll find out sooner or later. I mean it's not just as if Flynn were an ordinary student. He's one of the heroes of the School. When the boys discover he isn't going to graduate they'll wonder.'

'I realize that there will be talk but I see no reason for us to reveal the true cause of the young man's separation from this institution.' The operative verb puzzled Mr. Beckman until he remembered that the Principal had been, for a year or two during the war, a colonel in Washington and that he could still turn a military phrase with the best of the younger faculty men who had also served in the war.

'But *what* are we to say?' Mr. Beckman persisted. 'We shall have to give some excuse.'

'There is no occasion, Mr. Beckman, for us *ever* to give excuses,' said the Principal in a cool Star-Chamber voice. 'Besides, Commencement is only a week away and I am sure that if we all maintain a discreet silence the business will soon be forgotten. The only complication, as I've mentioned before, involves the Zenner Trophy. At the moment I'm tempted not to give it at all this year, but of course we'll have to see what our faculty committee digs up. . . . Anyway, that has nothing to do with the business at hand which, specifically, concerns the expulsion of Flynn, an unpleasant task traditionally performed by the Dean. In his absence, and he is absent, the sad duty must be performed by the faculty adviser involved.'

'Not by the Principal?'

'*Never* by the Principal,' said that officer, constructing a pile of papers in front of him as though to barricade himself even more securely against the sordid life of the School.

'I see. I don't suppose there is any chance of keeping him on? I mean of letting him graduate next week?' He felt that it was his duty to make this suggestion.

'Of course not! How could you suggest such a thing after what's happened? There were two witnesses and both were faculty members. Had there been only *one* witness we might perhaps . . .' The Principal paused, contemplating collusion, to no avail. He returned quickly to his original position, remarking that the morality of the thing was perfectly clear and that the crime and the punishment were both well-known and that there wouldn't have been this much discussion, if it had not been for that damned award. 'No, the boy has been expelled and that's that. I've already written to his parents.'

'Did you tell them what has happened? In detail?'

'I did,' said the Principal firmly. 'After all, he's their son and they should know everything. I wouldn't be doing my duty if I did not tell them.'

'Rather hard on him, don't you think?'

'Are *you* defending him?' The Principal reduced Mr. Beckman's momentary disaffection to total compliance with a single glance from agate eyes, eyes which had so often quelled student revolts, bullied the faculty, extorted endowments from the most brutal of millionaires.

'No, sir ... I only thought. ...' That was the end of that, thought Mr. Beckman gloomily, mumbling himself back into favour again.

'Very good,' said the Principal rising, ending the audience. 'You'll talk to him. Tell him that the faculty has unanimously expelled him and that the Zenner Trophy will be given to someone else. You might also mention the sorrow with which I personally learned of his ... activities and that I do not condemn him too much; rather, I pity him. It is a terrible handicap not to know right from wrong in such matters.'

'I shall tell him that, sir.'

'Good. ... Just what sort of young man *is* he? I've seen him play ball many times, of course ... a real champion ... but I never got to know him. On the few

occasions when we did meet he seemed perfectly ...
well-adjusted. He comes from a good home, too. Odd
that he should be such a marvellous athlete, all things
considered.'

'Yes, a marvellous athlete,' repeated Mr. Beckman.
This was apparently to be Flynn's epitaph; he tried to
translate it into Latin, but failed, unable to remember
the word for athlete.

'You never noticed anything unusual about him, did
you? Any clue which might, in retrospect, explain
what has happened.'

'No, sir. I'm sorry to say that I noticed nothing at
all.'

'Well, it's no fault of yours, or of the School's. These
things will happen.' The Principal sighed. Then: 'Drop
by my office around five ... if it's convenient.'

II

The morning was marvellously clear and bright, and
Mr. Beckman's weak eyes watered as he crossed the
lawn of the quadrangle, a vivid area of green in the
solemn light of noon. Students greeted him politely and
he responded vaguely, not seeing them, his eyes not yet
accustomed to the day. He blundered accurately across
the quadrangle to the library where he stood a moment,
blinking, until at last he could see that it was indeed a
lovely day and that the School looked most handsome.

The main buildings bordered the vast green lawn of
the quadrangle, a lawn marked with numerous gravelled
paths, designed with considerable geometric ingenuity

to allow, its architect had mistakenly supposed, for any possible crossing a student might want to make. Of the buildings on the quadrangle, the Administration Hall was the handsomest and the oldest; it was nearly old enough to be in fact what it was in facsimile: a colonial affair of red brick with a clock-tower and bell, a bell which irritated Mr. Beckman unreasonably. It rang at five minutes to every hour as well as on the hour from morning chapel until the last evening class. The bell rang now. Eleven o'clock. He had exactly one hour in which to 'separate' Flynn from the school he had so brilliantly adorned. A warm wind stirred the lilacs and, suddenly, he was frightened at what he had to do. He was not equipped to deal with mysteries. He had very early chosen the bland familiar for his domain and he had never before ventured into the dangerous interior of anothers' life: now, in a few moments, he must sack a temple, sow foreign earth with salt and rend a mystery. Half shutting his eyes against the blaze of sun, Mr. Beckman made his way to the rose-brick senior dormitory where Flynn and he both lived. Inside the building, he proceeded down the wax-smelling corridor, his tongue dry, his hands cold, panic insecurely leashed. At Flynn's door, he stopped. He knocked softly. Receiving no answer, he turned the knob and opened the door, praying the boy was gone.

Flynn had not gone. He was sitting on the edge of his bed, an open suitcase on the floor in front of him. He stood up when Mr. Beckman entered.

'Am I out?' he asked.

'Yes.' That was quick. For a moment, Mr. Beckman considered flight.

'I figured that would happen.' The boy sat down on the bed again. Mr. Beckman wondered what he should say next. Since nothing occurred to him, he seated himself at the desk by the window and assumed an expression of grave sympathy. The boy continued to pack his suitcase. A long moment of silence stretched taut Mr. Beckman's nerves. At last, he broke the silence.

'The Principal wanted me to tell you he is very sorry about what's happened.'

'Well, you tell him I'm sorry too,' said Flynn, looking up from his packing and, to Mr. Beckman's surprise, he was grinning. He seemed not at all shaken, Mr. Beckman remarked with wonder, examining him carefully. The eighteen-year-old Flynn was a well-constructed man of middle height, muscular but not burly like the other athletes: his freckled face was amiable and quite mature, his eyes dark blue; his hair, of no particular colour, was worn short, in a crew-cut. During the winter his hair had been longer and Mr. Beckman recalled that it had been quite curly, like the head of the young Dionysus.

He looked about the room, at the banners on the walls and at the calendar of partly-dressed girls, one for each month. In a corner was piled athletic equipment: football helmet, shoulder-pads, sweat-marked jerseys, shorts, tennis-racket – the tools of a serious career rather than the playthings of an energetic boy. No, he would never have known, never.

There was another long pause, but this time Mr. Beckman was more at ease even as he sensed his own position becoming less and less secure. 'I suppose,' he said, 'that you'll go on to college now.'

'Yes, I suppose I will. I got all the credits I need from high school, and the university back home wants me to play ball. I won't have any trouble getting in ... will I?'

'Oh no. No trouble at all, I'm sure.'

'*They* don't plan to make any trouble for me, do they?'

'Who do you mean by "they"?'

'The School. They aren't going to write to the university or anything like that, are they?'

'Oh, Heavens, no!' Mr. Beckman was relieved to have some good news, no matter how negative. 'Except for expelling you, they are doing nothing at all. Of course . . .' He paused, noticing that the other looked very grim.

'Of course what?'

'They have written to your parents.'

'Written to my parents *what*?'

'The . . . the whole business. It's customary, you understand. The Principal wrote the letter himself, today, this morning, as a matter of fact,' he added precisely, addressing his attention, as he always did in a crisis, to the periphery of the situation, to the incidental detail in the hopes that he might yet avoid involvement. But it was no use.

'Well, I'll be damned!' Flynn sat up straight, his large, square hands clenched into two useful and dangerous-looking fists. Mr. Beckman trembled. 'So he went and wrote everything, did he?' He stopped and hit the bed with his fist; the springs creaked. It was all very dramatic and Mr. Beckman sat up straight in his chair, raising one hand as though to defend himself.

'You must remember,' he said, his voice trembling, 'that the Principal was only doing his duty. You *were* caught, you know, and you *were* expelled. Don't you feel your parents deserve some sort of explanation?'

'No, I don't. Not like that, anyway. It's bad enough being kicked out without having that fool go and upset them. It's no way of getting back at me: I earn my own way. I can go to any school I want on a scholarship. Or I can turn pro tomorrow and make ten times the money that fool Principal makes. But why, I want to know, does somebody who doesn't even know me go out of his way to make such a mess for my family?'

'I'm sure it's not a deliberate persecution,' said Mr. Beckman dryly. 'And you should have thought of all that when ... when you did what you did. There *are* certain rules of conduct, you know, which must be obeyed and you obviously forgot ...'

'Oh, shut up!'

Mr. Beckman had a dizzy sense he was falling; only with great effort did he get to his feet, saying, shakily: 'If you're going to take that tone with me, Flynn, I see no point in ...'

'I'm sorry. I didn't mean it. Come on, sit down.' And Mr. Beckman sat down, his authority gone. He could no longer predict the direction this conversation would take, and he was actually relieved that the initiative was no longer his.

'You see how I feel, don't you?'

'Yes,' said Mr. Beckman. 'I do.' And unhappily he did. Not only was he sympathetic: he was partisan, hopelessly identified with the other. He shuddered at the thought of the meeting between son and parents and he tried to think of what would happen. Would she have a stroke? Would she weep? 'If there is anything I might do ...' he began.

Flynn smiled. 'No, I don't think there's anything to be done, thanks. I guess it was probably too much to expect ... I mean that they'd keep it quiet. But what about the rest of the school? Is the Principal going to get up in chapel and tell the whole story?'

'Oh no. His plan is to say nothing at all to the students. He's instructed the faculty to keep absolutely quiet.'

'Well, that's good news, but you know they're going to be wondering why Sawyer and I didn't graduate, why we left just a week before Commencement.' He paused; then: 'What're they going to do about the Trophy?'

'I don't know. Since they can't give it to you they're in rather a spot: if they re-award it, that will draw attention to the fact you've been expelled. I have a hunch they won't give it at all this year.' And Mr. Beckman chuckled, totally aligned against the School which until an hour ago he had so much admired and had so sincerely longed to serve.

'I guess that's their worry now,' said Flynn. 'Were they pretty shocked?'

'Who?'

'The faculty. You know: all the ones who knew me, like the coaches I worked with. What did they say?'

'No one said much of anything. I think they were all surprised. I mean you were just about the last person anyone would have expected to be involved . . . like this. I'm afraid *I* was rather surprised, too,' he added shyly, waiting.

But Flynn only snorted and looked out the window at the tower of the Administration Building, red brick against blue sky. At last he said: 'I guess there *is* something wrong with me, Mr. Beckman, because I can't for the life of me see what business it is of anyone else what I do.'

This was not at all what Mr. Beckman had anticipated; identified as he was with Flynn, he still found it difficult to accept the curious amorality of this attitude.

He took a firm line. 'You must realize,' he said, as gently as possible, 'that we are all guided by a system of conduct formulated and refined by many centuries. Should this system, or any important part of it, be destroyed, the whole complex structure of civilization would collapse.' Yet even as he said these familiar words, he realized that they were, in this case at least, irrelevant, and he noticed dispassionately that Flynn was not listening to him. He was standing over his athletic equipment, tossing the pieces he didn't want into a far corner of the room. Mr. Beckman enjoyed watching him move, for he never struck an ugly or a self-conscious attitude. 'And so you see,' he concluded to the boy's back, 'that when you do something as basically wrong as what you've done, you'll have all of organized society down on you and you'll be punished.'

'Maybe so,' Flynn straightened up, holding his armour, his weapons in his hands. 'But I still don't see why what I want to do should ever be anybody's business except my own. After all, it doesn't affect anybody else, does it?' Noisily he dumped the equipment into the open suitcase. Then he sat down on the bed again and looked at Mr. Beckman. 'You know I'd really like to get my hands on those two,' he said abruptly, scowling.

'They were only doing their duty. They had to report you.'

'I suppose I should have known they were suspicious in the first place . . . when I saw them last night, before I went up to Sawyer's room. They were hanging around the common-room, whispering. Sawyer thought there was something going on, but I said, so what.'

'And you were caught.'

'Yes.' He blushed and looked away. He seemed for

the first time very young; Mr. Beckman was compassionate.

'I gather,' he said slowly, allowing the other to regain his composure, 'that Sawyer went home.'

Flynn shook his head. 'No, he's over at the Inn, waiting for me. I figured they might want to question us, and I thought I'd better be the one who did the talking. He went over there first thing this morning.'

'What sort of boy is Sawyer? I don't think I've seen him around.'

Flynn looked at him with surprise. 'Of course you've seen him. He's on the track team. He's the best sprinter we got.'

'Oh yes, of course.' Mr. Beckman had not gone to any of the track meets. He had found that, after he'd attended the football and the baseball games, he didn't very much want to see the swimming team or the track team or even the school's celebrated basket-ball team.

'He's too small to play football, and besides he hasn't got the right temperament for a football player,' said Flynn professionally. 'He blows up too easily and he doesn't work out on a team . . .'

'I see. And you've been good friends for a long time?'

'Yes,' said Flynn, and he shut the suitcase with a snap.

'Where do you think you'll go now?' asked Mr. Beckman, obscurely anxious to prolong this interview.

'Back home, and it's not going to be much fun. I just hope my mother doesn't have a relapse or anything like that.'

'Where will Sawyer go?'

'Oh, he's coming on to the university with me. He's

got a high school diploma. He won't have any trouble getting in.'

'So then you aren't really very discouraged by all of this?'

'Why? I don't like what's happened, but then I don't see what I can do about it now.'

'You're very sensible. I'm afraid that if I'd been in your place I would have been most upset.'

'But you *wouldn't* have been in my place, would you, Mr. Beckman?' Flynn smiled.

'No, no, I don't suppose so,' said Mr. Beckman, aware that he had been abandoned long ago and that there was no one he could turn to now, no one he could confide in. He realized that he was quite alone, and he hated Flynn for reminding him of the long and tedious journey ahead, down an endless, chalk-smelling corridor where each forward step took him farther and farther from this briefly glimpsed design within a lilac day.

The bell rang. He stood up. It was time to go to class. 'I suppose you'll be leaving for Boston on the next train?'

Flynn nodded. 'Yes, I've got to take some books back to the library first; after that, I'll pick up Sawyer at the Inn. Then we go.'

'Well, good luck.' Mr. Beckman paused. 'I'm not so sure that, after all, any of this matters very much,' he said, in a last effort to console himself as well as the other.

'No, I don't suppose it does either.' Flynn was gentle. 'You've been very nice about this . . .'

'Don't mention it. By the way, if you like, I'll return any library books for you.'

'Thanks a lot.' Flynn took three books from the top of the desk and handed them to him.

Mr. Beckman hesitated. 'Do you ever get to Boston? I mean, do you think you'll come into town much after you enter the university?'

'Sure, I suppose so. I'll let you know and we might get together some week-end.'

'I should like that. Well, good-bye.' They shook hands and Mr. Beckman left the room, already late for class. Outside, he glanced at the titles of the books he was carrying: one was a volume of historical documents (required reading) and one was a mystery story. The third was a volume of Keats. Dazzled by sunlight, he crossed the quadrangle, aware there was nothing left that he could do.

1950

Erlinda and Mr. Coffin

I am a gentlewoman in middle life, and I have resided for a number of years at Key West, Florida, in a house which is a mere stone's throw from the naval station where the Presidents visit.

Before I recount, as nearly as I am able, what happened that terrible night at the Theatre-in-the-Egg, I feel that I should first give you some idea of myself and the circumstances to which Providence has seen fit to reduce me. I came originally from a Carolina family not much blessed with this world's goods, but whose lineage, if I may make the boast in all modesty, is of the highest. There is a saying that no legislature of the state could ever convene without the presence of a Slocum (my family name) in the Lower House, a lofty heritage, you must concede, and one which has done much to sustain me in my widowhood.

In olden times my social activities in this island city were multifarious, but since 1929 I have drawn in my horns, as it were, surrendering all my high offices in the various organizations with which our city abounds to one Marina Henderson, wife of our local shrimp magnate and a cultural force to be reckoned with in these parts not only because her means are ample, but because our celebrated Theatre-in-the-Egg is the child of her teeming imagination; she is its managing directress, star and some time authoress. Her productions have been uniformly well regarded since the proceeds go to charity. Then, too, the unorthodox arrangement of the theatre's interior has occasioned much interested comment, for the action, such as it is, takes place on an oval platform ('the yolk') about which the audience sits restively in camp chairs. There is no curtain, of course, and so the actors are forced to rush in and out, from lobby to yolk, traversing the aisles at a great rate.

Marina and I are good friends, however, even though we do not forgather as often as we once did: she now goes with a somewhat faster set than I, seeking out those of the winter residents who share her advanced views, while I keep to the small circle that I have known lo! these many years, since 1910, in fact, when I came to Key West from South Carolina, accompanied by my new husband, Mr. Bellamy Craig, who had accepted a position of some trust earlier that year with a bank which was to fail in '29, the year of his decease. But of course no such premonition marred our happiness when we set out, bag and baggage, to make our way in Key West.

I do not need to say that Mr. Craig was in every sense a gentleman, a devoted husband, and though our union was never fulfilled by the longed-for arrival of little ones, we managed, none the less, to have a happy home, one which was to end all too soon as I have intimated, for when he passed on in '29 I was left with but the tiniest of incomes, a mere pittance from my maternal grandmother in Carolina, and the house. Mr. Craig had unfortunately been forced, shortly before his death, to jettison his insurance policy, so I could not even clutch at that straw when my hour came.

I debated whether to go into business or to establish a refined luncheon-room or to seek a position with some established business house. I was not long in doubt, however, as to what course I should pursue. For, not being desirous of living anywhere but in my own home, I determined with some success, financially at least, to reorganize the house so that it might afford me an income through the distasteful but necessary expediency of giving shelter to paying guests.

Since the house is a commodious one, I have not done badly through the years and, in time, I have accustomed myself to this humiliating situation; then, too, I was sustained secretly by the vivid memory of my grandmother, Arabella Stuart Slocum, of Wayne County, who, when reduced from great wealth to penury by the war, maintained herself and children, widow that she was, by taking in laundry, mostly flat work, but still laundry. I will confess to you that there were times at night when I sat alone in my room hearkening to the heavy breathing of my guests, that I saw myself as a modern Arabella, living, as did she, in the face of adversity, inspired still by those high ideals we, she and I and all the Slocums, have held in common reverence since time immemorial in Wayne County.

And yet, in spite of every adversity, I should have said until recently that I had 'won through', that in twenty years as inn-keeper I had not once been faced with any ugliness, that I had been remarkably fortunate in my selection of paying guests, recruiting them, as I did, from the ranks of those who have reached 'the age of discretion', as we used to say. But all of this must now be in the past tense, alas.

Late one Sunday morning, three months ago, I was in the parlour attempting with very little success to tune the piano. I used to be quite expert at tuning, but my ear is no longer true and I was, I confess, experiencing a certain frustration when the ringing of the door-bell interrupted my labours. Expecting certain of my late husband's relatives who had promised to break bread with me that day, I hastened to answer the door. It was not they, however: instead, a tall, thin gentleman in middle life, wearing the long short trousers affected over in Bermuda, stood upon my threshold and begged admittance.

As was my wont, I ushered him into the parlour, where we sat down on the two Victorian plush chairs Grandmother Craig left me in her will. I asked him in what way I might be of service to him, and he intimated that rumour had it I entertained guests on a paying basis. I told him that he had not been misinformed and that, by chance, I had one empty room left, which he asked to see.

The room pleased him and, if I say so myself, it is attractively furnished with original copies of Chippendale and Regency, bought many years ago when, in the full flush of our prosperity, Mr. Craig and I furnished our nest with objects not only useful but ornamental. There are two big windows in this room: one on the south and the other on the west. From the south window there is a fine view of the ocean, only partly obliterated by a structure of pink stucco called the 'New Arcadia Motel'.

'This will do very well,' said Mr. Coffin (he had very soon confided his name to me). But then he paused, and I did not dare meet his gaze, for I thought that he was about to mention the root of all evil and, as always, I was ill at ease, for I have never been able to enact the role of business-woman without a certain shame, a distress which often-times communicates itself to the person with whom I must deal, causing no end of confusion for us both. But it was not of money that he wished to speak. If only it had been! If only we had gone no further in our dealings with one another. 'To call

back yesterday,' as the poet observed, 'bid time return!'
But it was not to be, and wishing cannot change the past,
He spoke then of *her*.

'You see, Mrs. Craig, I must tell you that I am not
alone.' Was it his English accent which gave me a sense
of false security, created a fool's paradise wherein I was
to dwell blissfully until the rude awakening? I cannot
tell. Suffice it to say I trusted him.

'Not alone?' I queried. 'Have you some companion
who travels with you? A gentleman?'

'No, Mrs. Craig, a young lady, my ward . . . a Miss
Lopez.'

'But I fear, Mr. Coffin, that I have only the one room
free at the moment.'

'Oh, she can stay with me, Mrs. Craig, in this room.
You see, she is only eight.' Both of us had a good laugh
and my suspicions, such as they had been, were instantly
allayed. He asked me if I could find him a cot, and I said
of course, nothing could be more simple; and then, correctly estimating the value of the room from the sign on
the door, he gave me a week's rent in cash, demonstrating such delicacy of feeling by his silence at this juncture
that I found myself much prejudiced in his favour. We
parted then on excellent terms, and I instructed my girl-
of-all-work to place a cot in the room and to dust carefully. I even had her supply him with the better bath
towels, after which I went in to dinner with my cousins
who had meanwhile arrived, ravenously hungry.

Not until the next morning did I see Mr. Coffin's
ward. She was seated in the parlour looking at an old
copy of *Vogue*. 'Good morning,' she said, and, as I entered the room, she rose and curtsied, very prettily I
must admit. 'I am Erlinda Lopez, the ward of Mr.
Coffin.'

'I am Mrs. Bellamy Craig, your hostess,' I answered with equal ceremony.

'Do you mind if I look at your magazines?'

'Certainly not,' I said, containing all the while my surprise not only at her good manners and grown-up ways, but at the unexpected fact that Miss Lopez was of an unmistakable dusky hue, in short a Dark Latin. Now I must say that, although I am in many ways typical of my age and class, I have no great prejudice on the subject of race. Our family, even in their slave-holding days, were always good to their people, and once as a child when I allowed the forbidden word 'nigger' to pass my lips I was forced to submit to a thorough oral cleansing by my mother, with a cake of strong soap. Yet I am, after all, a Southern woman, and I do not choose to receive people of colour in my own home: call it intolerant, old-fashioned, or what you will, it is the way I am. Imagine then what thoughts coursed through my startled brain! What was I to do? Having accepted a week's rent was I not morally obligated to maintain both Mr. Coffin and his ward in my house? At least until the week was up? In an agony of indecision, I left the parlour and went straight to Mr. Coffin. He received me cordially.

'Have you met Erlinda yet, Mrs. Craig?'

'I have indeed, Mr. Coffin.'

'I think her quite intelligent. She speaks French, Spanish and English fluently and she has a reading knowledge of Italian.'

'A gifted child I am sure, but *really*, Mr. Coffin . . .'

'Really what, Mrs. Craig?'

'I mean I am not *blind*. How can she be your ward? She is . . . coloured!' I had said it and I was relieved: the fat was in the fire; there was no turning back.

'Many people are, Mrs. Craig.'

'I am aware of that, Mr. Coffin, but I had not assumed that your ward was to be counted among that number.'

'Then, Mrs. Craig, if it offends your sensibilities, we will seek lodgings elsewhere.' Oh, what insane impulse made me reject this gesture of his? What flurry of *noblesse oblige* in my breast caused me suddenly to refuse even to entertain such a contingency! I do not know; suffice it to say, I ended by bidding him remain with his ward as long as he should care to reside beneath my roof, on a paying basis.

When the first week was up I must confess that I was more pleased than not with my reckless decision, for, although I did not mention to my friends that I was giving shelter to a person of colour, I found Erlinda, none the less, to be possessed of considerable charm and personality, and I spent at least an hour every day in her company, at first from a sense of duty, but, finally, from a very real pleasure in her conversation which, when I recall it now (the pleasure, I mean), causes my cheeks to burn with shame.

I discovered in our talks that she was, as I had suspected, an orphan and that she had travelled extensively in Europe and Latin America, wintering in Amalfi, summering in Venice, and so on. Not of course that I for one moment believed these stories, but they were so charming and indicated such a fund of information that I was only too pleased to listen to her descriptions of the Lido, and her recitations from Dante, in flawless Italian or what I took to be Italian, since I have never studied other tongues. But, as I have said, I took her tales with the proverbial grain of salt and, from time to time, I chatted with Mr. Coffin, gleaning from him – as much as I was able without appearing to pry – the story of Erlinda's life.

She was the child of a Cuban prize-fighter who had toured Europe many times, taking Erlinda with him on his trips, showering her with every luxury and engaging tutors for her instruction, with a particular emphasis on languages, world literature and deportment. Her mother had died a few months after Erlinda was born. Mr. Coffin, it seems, had known the prize-fighter for several years, and since he, Mr. Coffin, was English, a friendship between them was possible. They were, I gathered, very close, and since Mr. Coffin had independent means they were able to travel together about Europe, Mr. Coffin eventually assuming responsibility for Erlinda's education.

This idyllic existence ended abruptly a year ago when Lopez was killed in the ring by a Sicilian named Balbo. It appears that this Balbo was not a sportsman, and that shortly before the fight he had contrived to secrete a section of lead pipe in his right boxing-glove, enabling him to crush Lopez's skull in the first round. Needless to say, the scandal which ensued was great. Balbo was declared middleweight champion of Sicily, and Mr. Coffin, after protesting to the authorities, who turned a deaf ear to him, departed, taking Erlinda with him.

As my friends will testify, I am easily moved by a tale of misfortune and, for a time, I took this motherless tyke to my heart. I taught her portions of the Bible which she had not studied before (Mr. Coffin, I gather, was a free-thinker), and she showed me the scrap-books she and Mr. Coffin had kept of her father's career as a pugilist – and a handsome young man he was, if photographs were to be believed.

Consequently, when a new week rolled around and

the period of probation, as it were, was up, I extended them the hospitality of my home indefinitely; soon a pattern of existence took shape. Mr. Coffin would spend most of his days looking for shells (he was a collector and, I am assured by certain authorities, the discoverer of a new type of pink-lipped conch), while Erlinda would remain indoors, reading, playing the piano or chatting with me about one thing or the other. She won my heart, and not only mine but those of my friends who had soon discovered, as friends will, the unusual combination I was sheltering. But my fears were proved to be groundless, a little to my surprise, for the ladies of my acquaintance are not noted for their tolerance: yet Erlinda enchanted them all with her conversation and saucy ways. Especially Marina Henderson, who was not only immediately attracted to Erlinda personally, but, and this I must say startled me, professed to see in the child Thespian qualities of the highest order.

'Mark my words, Louise Craig,' she said to me one afternoon when we were sitting in the parlour waiting for Erlinda, who had gone upstairs to fetch one of the scrap-books, 'that child will be a magnificent actress. Have you listened to her voice?'

'Since I have been constantly in her company for nearly three weeks, I could hardly *not* have heard it,' I responded dryly.

'I mean its timbre. The inflexion . . . it's like velvet, I tell you!'

'But how can she be an actress in this country when ₃ . . well, let us say the opportunities open to one of her ₃ . . *characteristics* are limited to occasional brief appearances as a lady's maid?'

'That's beside the point,' said Marina, and she rattled on as she always does when something new has hit her fancy, ignoring all difficulties, courting disaster with a fine show of high spirits and bad judgment.

'Perhaps the child has no intention of exploiting her dramatic gifts?' I suggested, unconsciously wishing to avert disaster.

'Nonsense,' said Marina, staring at herself in the tilted Victorian mirror over the fire-place, admiring that remarkable red hair of hers which changes its shade from season to season, from decade to decade, like the leaves in autumn. 'I shall talk to her about it this afternoon.'

'You have something in mind then? Some role?'

'I have,' said Marina slyly.

'Not . . .?'

'Yes!' Needless to say, I was astonished. For several months our island city had been agog with rumours concerning Marina's latest work, an adaptation of that fine old classic *Camille*, executed in blank verse and containing easily the finest part for an actress within memory, the title role. Competition for this magnificent part had been keen, but the demands of the role were so great that Marina had hesitated to entrust it to any of the regular stars, including herself.

'But this will never do!' I exclaimed; my objections were cut short, however, by the appearance of Erlinda, and when next I spoke the deed was done and Erlinda Lopez had been assigned the stellar role in Marina Henderson's *Camille*, based on the novel by Dumas and the screen-play by Miss Zoe Akins.

It is curious, now that I think of it, how everyone accepted as a matter of course that Erlinda should interpret an adult Caucasian woman from Paris whose private life was not what it should have been. I can only say, in this regard, that those who heard her read for the

part, and I was one of them, were absolutely stunned by
the emotions she brought to those risqué lines, as well as
by the thrilling quality of her voice which, in the word
of Mr. Hamish, the newspaperman, was 'golden'. That
she was only eight and not much over three feet tall
disturbed no one, for, as Marina said, it is *presence*
which matters on the stage, even in the 'Theatre-in-the-
Egg': make-up and lighting would do the rest. The only
difficulty, as we saw it, was the somewhat ticklish problem of race, but since this is a small community with
certain recognized social arbiters, good form prevents
the majority from questioning too finely the decisions of
our leaders, and as Marina occupies a position of
peculiar eminence among us, there was, as far as I
know, no grumbling against her bold choice. Marina
herself, by far our most accomplished actress, certainly
our most indefatigable one, assigned herself the minor
role of Camille's confidante Cecile. Knowing Marina as
I do, I was somewhat startled that she had allowed the
stellar role to go to someone else, but then recalling that
she was, after all, directress and authoress, I could see
that she would undoubtedly have been forced to spread
herself too thin had she undertaken such an arduous
task.

Now I do not know precisely what went on during the
rehearsals. I was never invited to attend them, and although I felt I had some connection with the production,
Erlinda having been my discovery in the first place, I
made no demur and sought in no way to interfere. Word
came to me, however, that Erlinda was magnificent.

I was seated in the parlour one afternoon with Mr.
Coffin, sewing some lace on a tea-gown our young star
was to wear in the first scene, when Erlinda burst into
the room.

'What is the matter, child?' I asked as she hastened to bury her head in her guardian's lap, great sobs racking her tiny frame.

'Marina!' came the muffled complaint. 'Marina Henderson is a ...!' Shocked as I was by the child's cruel observation, I could not but, in my heart of hearts, agree that there was some truth to this crushing estimate of my old friend's character. None the less, it was my duty to defend her, and I did, as best I could, recounting relevant episodes from her life to substantiate my defence. But before I could even get to the quite interesting story of how she happened to marry Mr. Henderson, I was cut short by a tirade of abuse against my oldest friend, an attack inspired, it soon developed, by a quarrel they had had over Erlinda's interpretation of her part, a quarrel which had ended in Marina's assumption of the role of Camille while presenting Erlinda with the terrible choice of either withdrawing from the company entirely or else accepting the role of Cecile, hitherto played by the authoress herself.

Needless to say, we were all in a state of uproar for twenty-four hours. Erlinda would neither eat nor sleep. According to Mr. Coffin she paced the floor all night, or at least when he had slipped off to the Land of Nod she was still pacing, and when he awakened early the next morning she was seated bitterly by the window, haggard and exhausted, the bedclothes on her cot undisturbed.

I counselled caution, knowing the influence Marina has in this town, and my advice was duly followed when, with broken heart but proud step, Erlinda returned to the boards in the part of Cecile. Had I but known the fruit of my counsel I would have torn my tongue out by the roots rather than advise Erlinda as I did. But what is done is done. In my defence, I can only say that I acted from ignorance and not from malice.

The opening night saw as brilliant an assemblage as you could hope to see in Key West. The cream of our local society was there as well as several of the President's retinue and a real playwright from New York. You have probably heard many conflicting stories about that night. Everyone in the state of Florida now claims to have been present, and, to hear the stories some of the people who were there tell, you would think they had been a hundred miles away from the theatre that fateful night. In any event, *I* was there in my white mesh over peacock blue foundation, carrying the imitation egret fan that I have had for twenty years, an anniversary gift from Mr. Craig.

Mr. Coffin and I sat together, both of us excited to fever pitch by the long-awaited début of our young star. The audience, too, seemed to have sensed that something remarkable was about to happen, for when, in the middle of the first scene, Erlinda appeared in a gown of orchid-coloured tulle, they applauded loudly.

*   *   *

As we took our seats for the fifth and final act we were both aware that Erlinda had triumphed. Not even in the movies have I ever seen such a performance! Or heard such a magnificent voice! Poor Marina sounded like a Memphis frump by comparison, and it was obvious to all who knew our authoress that she was in a rage at being outshone in her own production.

Now, in the last act of Marina's *Camille* there is a particularly beautiful and touching scene where Camille is lying on a chaise-longue, wearing a flowing negligée of white rayon. There is a table beside her on which is set a silver candelabra, containing six lighted tapers, a bowl of paper camellias and some Kleenex. The scene began something like this:

'Oh, will he never come? Tell me, sweet Cecile, do you not see his carriage approaching from the window?' Cecile (Erlinda) pretends to look out a window and answers: 'There is no one in the street but a little old man selling the evening newspapers.'

The language, as you see, is poetic and much the best writing Marina has done to date. Then there is a point in the action, the great moment of the play, when Camille (that's not the character's real name, I understand, but Marina called her that so as not to confuse the audience), after a realistic fit of coughing, rises up on her elbows and exclaims: 'Cecile! It grows dark. He has not come. Light more tapers, do you hear me? I need more light!'

Then it happened. Erlinda picked up the candelabra and held it aloft for a moment, a superhuman effort since it was larger than she; then, taking aim, she hurled it at Marina, who was instantly ignited. Pandemonium broke loose in the theatre! Marina, a pillar of fire, streaked down the aisle and into the night: she was subdued at last in the street by two policemen who managed to put out the blaze, after which they removed her to the hospital where she now resides, undergoing at this moment her twenty-fourth skin graft.

Erlinda remained on the stage long enough to give *her* reading of Camille's great scene which, according to those few who were close enough to hear it, was indeed splendid. Then, the scene finished, she left the theatre and before either Mr. Coffin or I could get to her, she was arrested on a charge of assault and battery, and incarcerated.

My story, however, is not yet ended. Had this been all
I might have said: let bygones be bygones. The mis-
creant is only a child, and Marina *did* do her an injury,
but during the subsequent investigation it was revealed
to a shocked public that Erlinda had been legally married to Mr. Coffin in the Reformed Eritrean Church of
Cuba several months before and a medical examination
proved, or so the defence claims, that Erlinda is actually
forty-one years old, a dwarf, the mother and not the
daughter of the pugilist Lopez. To date the attendant
legal complications have not yet been unravelled to the
court's satisfaction.

Fortunately, at this time, I was able to avail myself of
a much-needed vacation in Carolina where I resided
with kin in Wayne County until the trouble in Key
West had abated somewhat.

I now visit Marina regularly, and she is beginning to
look more or less like her old self, even though her hair
and eyebrows are gone for good and she will have to
wear a wig when she finally rises from her bed of pain.
Only once has she made any reference to Erlinda in my
presence, and that was shortly after my return from the
north when she remarked that the child had been tem-
peramentally all wrong for the part of Camille and that
if she had it to do over again, everything considered, she
would still have fired her.

1951

Pages from an Abandoned Journal

I

30th April, 1948

After last night, I was sure they wouldn't want to see me again but evidently I was wrong because this morning I had a call from Steven – he spells it with a 'v' – asking me if I would like to come to a party at Elliott Magren's apartment in the Rue du Bac. I should have said no but I didn't. It's funny: when I make up my mind *not* to do something I always end up by doing it, like meeting Magren, like seeing any of these people again, especially after last night. Well, I guess it's experience. What was it Pascal wrote? I don't remember what Pascal wrote – another sign of weakness: I should look it up when I don't remember; the book is right here on the table, but the thought of leafing through all those pages is discouraging so I pass on.

Anyway, now that I'm in Paris I've got to learn to be more adaptable and I do think, all in all, I've handled myself pretty well ... until last night in the bar when I told everybody off. I certainly never thought I'd see Steven again: that's why I was so surprised to get his call this morning. Is he still hopeful after what I said? I can't see how. I was *ruthlessly* honest. I said I wasn't interested, that I didn't mind what other people did, etc., just as long as they left me alone, that I was getting married in the autumn when I got back to the States (WRITE HELEN) and that I don't go in for any of that, never did and never will. I also told him in no uncertain terms that it's very embarrassing for a grown man to be treated like some idiot girl surrounded by a bunch of

seedy, middle-aged Don Juans trying to get their hooks
into her . . . him. Anyway, I really let him have it before
I left. Later, I felt silly but I was glad to go on record
like that once and for all: now we know where we stand
and if they're willing to accept me on *my* terms, the way
I am, then there's no reason why I can't see them sometimes. That's really why I agreed to meet Magren who
sounds very interesting from what everybody says,
and everybody talks a lot about him, at least in those
circles which must be the largest and busiest circles
in Paris this spring. Well, I shouldn't complain: this is
the Bohemian life I wanted to see. It's just that there
aren't many girls around, for fairly obvious reasons.
In fact, except for running into Hilda Devendorf
at American Express yesterday, I haven't seen an
American girl to talk to in the three weeks I've been
here.

My day: after the phone call from Steven, I worked
for two and a half hours on Nero and the Civil Wars. I
wish sometimes I'd picked a smaller subject for a doctorate, not that I don't like the period, but having to
learn German to read a lot of books all based on sources
available to anybody is depressing: I could do the whole
thing from Tacitus but that would be cheating, no
bibliography, no footnotes, no scholastic quarrels to
record and judge between. Then, though the day was
cloudy, I took a long walk across the river to the
Tuileries where the gardens looked fine. Just as I was
turning home into the Rue de l'Université it started to
rain and I got wet. At the desk Madame Revenel told me
Hilda had called. I called her back and she said she was
going to Deauville on Friday to visit some people who
own a hotel and why didn't I go too? I said I might and
wrote down her address. She's a nice girl. We were in

high school together back in Toledo; I lost track of her
when I went to Columbia.

Had dinner here in the dining-room (veal, french fried
potatoes, salad and something like a pie but very good. I
like the way Madame Revenel cooks). She talked to me
all through dinner, very fast, which is good because the
faster she goes the less chance you have to translate in
your head. The only other people in the dining-room
were the Harvard professor and his wife. They both
read while they ate. He's supposed to be somebody important in the English Department, but I've never heard
of him. Paris is like that: everyone's supposed to be
somebody important, only you've never heard of them.
The Harvard professor was reading a mystery story and
his wife was reading a life of Alexander Pope.

I got to the Rue du Bac around ten-thirty. Steven
opened the door, yelling: 'The beautiful Peter!' This was
about what I expected. Anyway, I got into the room
quickly . . . if they're drunk they're apt to try to kiss you
and there was no point in getting off on the wrong foot
again, but luckily he didn't try. He showed me through
the apartment, four big rooms one opening off another;
here and there an old chair was propped against a wall
and that was all the furniture there was till we got to the
last room where, on a big bed with a torn canopy, Elliott
Magren lay, fully dressed, propped up by pillows. All
the lamps had red shades. Over the bed was a painting
of a nude man, the work of a famous painter I'd never
heard of (read Berenson!)

There were about a dozen men in the room, most of
them middle-aged and wearing expensive narrow suits. I
recognized one or two of them from last night. They
nodded to me but made no fuss. Steven introduced me
to Elliott who didn't move from the bed when he shook

hands; instead, he pulled me down beside him. He had a surprisingly powerful grip, considering how pale and slender he is. He told Steven to make me a drink. Then he gave me a long serious look and asked me if I wanted a pipe of opium. I said I didn't take drugs and he said nothing which was unusual: as a rule they give you a speech about how good it is for you, or else they start defending themselves against what they feel is moral censure. Personally, I don't mind what other people do. As a matter of fact, I think all this is very interesting and I sometimes wonder what the gang back in Toledo would think if they could've seen me in a Left-Bank Paris apartment with a male prostitute who takes drugs. I thought of those college boys who sent T. S. Eliot the record 'You've Come a Long Way From St. Louis.'

Before I describe what happened, I'd better write down what I've heard about Magren, since he is already a legend in Europe, at least in these circles. First of all, he is not very handsome. I don't know what I'd expected but something glamorous, like a movie star. He is about five foot ten and weighs about a hundred and sixty pounds. He has dark straight hair that falls over his forehead; his eyes are black. The two sides of his face don't match, like Oscar Wilde's, though the effect is not as disagreeable as Wilde's face must've been from the photographs. Because of drugs, he is unnaturally pale. His voice is deep and his accent is still Southern; he hasn't picked up that phoney English accent so many Americans do after five minutes over here. He was born in Galveston, Texas about thirty-six years ago. When he was sixteen he was picked up on the beach by a German baron who took him to Berlin with him. (I always wonder about details in a story like this: what did his parents say about a stranger walking off with their son?

Was there a scene? Did they know what was going on?)
Elliott then spent several years in Berlin during the
twenties which were the great days, or what these
people recall now as the great days. I gather the German
boys were affectionate: it all sounds pretty disgusting.
Then Elliott had a fight with the baron and he walked,
with no money, nothing but the clothes he was wearing,
from Berlin to Munich. On the outskirts of Munich, a
big car stopped and the chauffeur said that the owner of
the car would like to give him a lift. The owner turned
out to be a millionaire ship-owner from Egypt, very fat
and old. He was intrigued with Elliott and he took him
on a yachting tour of the Mediterranean. But Elliott
couldn't stand him and when the ship got to Naples,
Elliott and a Greek sailor skipped ship together after
first stealing two thousand dollars from the Egyptian's
state-room. They went to Capri where they moved into
the most expensive hotel and had a wonderful time until
the money ran out and the sailor deserted Elliott for a
rich American woman. Elliott was about to be taken off
to jail for not paying his bill when Lord Glenellen, who
was just checking into the hotel, saw him and told the
police to let him go, that *he* would pay his bill. Here
again: how would Glenellen know that it would be
worth his while to help this stranger? I mean you can't
tell by looking at him that Elliott is queer. Suppose he
hadn't been? Well, maybe that soldier I met on Oki-
nawa the night of the hurricane was right: they can
always tell about each other, like Masons. Glenellen
kept Elliott for a number of years. They went to England together and Elliott rose higher and higher in
aristocratic circles until he met the late King Basil who
was then a prince. Basil fell in love with him and Elliott
went to live with him until Basil became king. They

didn't see much of each other after that because the war started and Elliott went to California to live. Basil died during the war, leaving Elliott a small trust fund which is what he lives on now. In California, Elliott got interested in Vedanta and tried to stop taking drugs and lead a quiet, if not a normal, life. People say he was all right for several years, but when the war ended he couldn't resist going back to Europe. Now he does nothing but smoke opium, his courtesan life pretty much over. This has been a long account, but I'm glad I got it all down because the story is an interesting one and I've heard so many bits and pieces of it since I got here that it helps clarify many things just writing this down in my journal. It is now past four o'clock and I've got a hangover already from the party but I'm going to finish, just as discipline. I never seem to finish anything which is a bad sign, God knows.

While I was sitting with Elliott on the bed Steven brought him his opium pipe, a long painted wooden affair with a metal chimney. Elliott inhaled deeply, holding the smoke in his lungs as long as he could; then he exhaled the pale medicinal-scented smoke, and started to talk. I can't remember a word he said. I was aware, though, that this was probably the most brilliant conversation I'd ever heard. It might have been the setting, which was certainly provocative, or maybe I'd inhaled some of the opium which put me in a receptive mood, but, no matter the cause, I sat listening to him, fascinated, not wanting him to stop. As he talked, he kept his eyes shut and I suddenly realized why the lamp-shades were red: the eyes of drug addicts are hypersensitive to light; whenever he opened his eyes he would blink painfully and the tears would streak his face, glistening like small watery rubies in the red light. He told me about himself, pretending to be a modern Candide, simple and bewildered, but actually he must have been quite different, more calculating, more resourceful. Then he asked me about myself and I couldn't tell if he was really interested or not because his eyes were shut and it's odd talking to someone who won't look at you. I told him about Ohio and high school and the university and now Columbia and the doctorate I'm trying to get in History and the fact I want to teach, to marry Helen. But as I talked I couldn't help but think how dull my life must sound to Elliott. I cut it short. I couldn't compete with him, and didn't want to. Then he asked me if I'd see him some evening, alone, and I said I would like to but – and this was completely on the spur of the moment – I said I was going down to Deauville the next day, with a girl. I wasn't sure he'd heard any of this because at that moment Steven pulled me off the bed and tried to make me dance with him, which I wouldn't do, to the amusement of the others. Then Elliott went to sleep, so I sat and talked for a while with an interior decorator from New York and, as usual, I was floored by the amount these people know: painting, music, literature, architecture – where do they learn it all? I sit like a complete idiot, supposedly educated, almost a Ph.D., while they talk circles around me: Fragonard, Boucher, Leonore Fini, Gropius, Sacheverell, Sitwell, Ronald Firbank, Jean Genet, Jean Giono, Jean Cocteau, Jean Brown's body lies a'mouldering in Robert Graves. God damn them all. I have the worst headache and outside it's dawn. Remember to write Helen, call Hilda about Deauville, study German two hours tomorrow instead of one, start boning up on Latin again, read Berenson, get a book on modern art (what book?), read Firbank. . . .

II

21st May, 1948

Another fight with Hilda. This time about religion. She's a Christian Scientist. It all started when she saw me taking two aspirins this morning because of last night's hangover. She gave me a lecture on Christ, Scientist and we had a long fight about God on the beach (which was wonderful today, not too many people, not too hot). Hilda looked more than ever like a great golden seal. She is a nice girl, but like so many who go to Bennington feels she must continually be alert to the life about her. I think tonight we'll go to bed together. Remember to get suntan oil, change money at hotel, finish Berenson, study German grammar! See if there's a Firbank in a paper edition.

22nd May, 1948

It wasn't very successful last night. Hilda kept talking all the time which slows me down, also she is a good deal softer than she looks and it was like sinking into a feather mattress. I don't think she has bones, only elastic webbing. Well, maybe it'll be better tonight. She seemed pleased but then I think she likes the idea better than the actual thing. She told me she had her first affair at fourteen. We had another argument about God. I told her the evidence was slight, etc., but she said evidence had nothing to do with faith. She told me a long story about how her mother had cancer last year but wouldn't see a doctor and the cancer went away. I didn't have the heart to tell her that mother's days are unpleasantly numbered. We had a wonderful dinner at that place on the sea, lobster, *moules*. Write Helen.

24th May, 1948

A fight with Hilda, this time about Helen whom she
hardly knows. She felt that Helen was pretentious. I
said: 'Who isn't?'. She said many people weren't. I said:
'Name me one.' She said *she* wasn't pretentious. I then
told her all the pretentious things she'd said in the past
week, starting with that discussion about the import-
ance of an aristocracy and ending with atonalism. She
then told me all the pretentious things I'd said, things I
either didn't remember saying or she had twisted
around. I got so angry I stalked out of her room and
didn't go back: just as well. Having sex with her is about
the dullest pastime I can think of. I went to my room
and read Tacitus in Latin, for practice.

My sunburn is better but I think I've picked up some
kind of liver trouble. Hope it's not jaundice: a burning
feeling right where the liver is.

25th May, 1948

Hilda very cool this morning when we met on the beach.
Beautiful day. We sat on the sand a good yard between
us, and I kept thinking how fat she's going to be in a few
years, only fit for child-bearing. I also thought happily
of those agonizing 'painless' childbirths she'd have to
endure because of Christian Science. We were just beginning to quarrel about the pronunciation of a French
word when Elliott Magren appeared – the last person in
the world I expected to see at bright noon on that beach.
He was walking slowly, wearing sun-glasses and a pair
of crimson trunks. I noticed with surprise how smooth
and youthful his body was, like a boy. I don't know
what I'd expected: something gaunt and hollowed out I
suppose, wasted by drugs. He came up to me as though
he'd expected to meet me right where I was. We shook

hands and I introduced him to Hilda who fortunately missed the point to him from the very beginning. He was as charming as ever. It seems he had to come to Deauville alone – he hated the sun but liked the beach – and, in answer to the golden Hilda's inevitable question, no, he was not married. I wanted to tell her everything, just to see what would happen, to break for a moment that beaming complacency, but I didn't.

                                    27th May, 1948

Well, this afternoon, Hilda decided it was time to go back to Paris. I carried her bag to the station and we didn't quarrel once. She was pensive but I didn't offer the usual small change for her thoughts. She didn't mention Elliott and I have no idea how much she suspects; in any case, it's none of her business, none of mine either. I think, though, I was nearly as shocked as she was when he came back to the hotel this morning with that fourteen-year-old boy. We were sitting on the terrace having coffee when Elliott, who must've got up very early, appeared with this boy. Elliott even introduced him to us and the little devil wasn't faintly embarrassed, assuming, I guess, that we were interested in him, too. Then Elliott whisked him off to his room and, as Hilda and I sat in complete silence, we could hear from Elliott's room on the first floor the hoarse sound of the boy's laughter. Not long after, Hilda decided to go back to Paris.

Wrote a long letter to Helen, studied Latin grammar. I'm more afraid of my Latin than of anything else in either the written or the orals: can't seem to concentrate, can't retain all those irregular verbs. Well, I've come this far. I'll probably get through all right.

28th May, 1948

This morning I knocked on Elliott's door around eleven o'clock. He'd asked me to pick him up on my way to the beach. When he shouted 'Come in!' I did and found both Elliott and the boy on the floor together, stark naked, putting together a Meccano set. Both were intent on building an intricate affair with wheels and pulleys, a blueprint between them. I excused myself hurriedly, but Elliott told me to stay, they'd be finished in a moment. The boy, who was the colour of a terra-cotta pot, gave me a wicked grin. Then Elliot, completely unself-conscious, jumped to his feet and pulled on a pair of trunks and a shirt. The boy dressed too, and we went out on the beach where the kid left us. I was blunt. I asked Elliott if this sort of thing wasn't very dangerous and he said, yes it probably was but life was short and he was afraid of nothing, except drugs. He told me then that he had an electrical shock treatment at a clinic shortly before I'd first met him. Now, at last, he was off opium and he hoped it was a permanent cure. He described the shock treatment, which sounded terrible. Part of his memory was gone: he could recall almost nothing of his childhood. Yet he was blithe even about this: after all, he believed only in the present. . . . Then when I asked him if he always went in for young boys he said, yes, and made a joke about how, having lost all memory of his own child-hood, he would have to live out a new one with some boy.

29th May, 1948

I had a strange conversation with Elliott last night. André went home to his family at six and Elliott and I had an early dinner on the terrace. A beautiful evening: the sea green in the last light, a new moon. Eating fresh sole from the Channel, I told Elliott all about Jimmy, told him things I myself had nearly forgotten, had wanted to forget. I told him how it had started at twelve and gone on, without plan or thought or even acknowledgment until, at seventeen, I went to the army and he to the Marines and a quick death. After the army, I met Helen and forgot him completely; his death, like Elliott's shock treatment, took with it all memory, a thousand summer days abandoned on a coral island. I can't think now why on earth I told Elliott about Jimmy; not that I'm ashamed but it was after all something intimate, something nearly forgotten. Anyway, when I finished, I sat there in the dark, not daring to look at Elliott, shivering as all in a rush the warmth left the sand about us and I had that terrible feeling I always have when I realize too late I've said too much. Finally, Elliott spoke. He gave me a strange disjointed speech about life and duty to oneself and how the moment is all one has and how dishonourable to cheat oneself of that. I'm not sure that he said anything very useful or very original but sitting there in the dark, listening, his words had a peculiar urgency for me and I felt, in a way, that I was listening to an oracle.

1st June, 1948

Shortly before lunch, the police came and arrested Elliott. Luckily, I was down on the beach and missed the whole thing. The hotel's in an uproar and the manager's behaving like a mad man. It seems André stole Elliott's camera. His parents found it and asked him where he got it. He wouldn't tell. When they threatened him he said Elliott gave him the camera and then, to make this story credible, he told them that Elliott had tried to seduce him. The whole sordid business then proceeded logically: parents to police, police to Elliott, arrest. I sat down shakily on the terrace and wondered what to do. I was ... I am frightened. While I was sitting there, a gendarme came out on the terrace and told me Elliott wanted to see me, in prison. Meanwhile, the gendarme wanted to know what I knew about Mr. Magren. It was only too apparent what his opinion of me was: another *pédéraste américain.* My voice shook and my throat dried up as I told him I hardly knew Elliott; I'd only just met him; I knew nothing about his private life. The gendarme sighed and closed his note-book: the charges against Elliott were *très graves, très graves,* but I would be allowed to see him tomorrow morning. Then realizing I was both nervous and unco-operative, the gendarme gave me the address of the jail and left. I went straight to my room and packed. I didn't think twice. All I wanted was to get away from Deauville, from Elliott, from the crime ... and it *was* a crime, I'm sure of that. I was back in Paris in time for supper at the hotel.

4th June, 1948

Ran into Steven at the Café Flore and I asked him if there'd been any news of Elliott. Steven took the whole thing as a joke: yes, Elliott had called a mutual friend who was a lawyer and everything was all right. Money was spent; the charges were dropped and Elliott was staying on in Deauville for another week, doubtless to be near André. I was shocked but relieved to hear this. I'm not proud of my cowardice but I didn't want to be drawn into something I hardly understood.

Caught a glimpse of Hilda with some college boy, laughing and chattering as they left the brasserie across the street. I stepped behind a kiosk, not wanting Hilda to see me. Write Helen. See the doctor about wax in ears, also liver. Get tickets for Roland Petit ballet.

.

III

26th December, 1953

The most hideous hangover! How I hate Christmas, especially this one. Started out last night at the Caprice where the management gave a party, absolutely packed. The new room is quite stunning, to my surprise: black walls, white driftwood but not artsy-craftsy, starlight effect for the ceiling. Only the upholstery is really *mauvais goût*: tufted velveteen in SAFFRON! But then Piggy has no sense of colour and why somebody didn't stop him I'll never know. All the tired old faces were there. Everyone was going to the ballet except me and there was all the usual talk about who was sleeping with whom, such a bore. I mean who cares who ... whom dancers sleep with? Though somebody did say that Niellsen was having an affair with Dr. Bruckner which is something of a surprise considering what a mess there was at Fire Island last summer over just that. Anyway, I drank too much vodka martinis and, incidentally, met Robert Gammadge the English playwright who isn't at all attractive though he made the biggest play for me. He's supposed to be quite dreary but makes tons of money. He was with that awful Dickie Mallory whose whole life is devoted to meeting celebrities, even the wrong ones. Needless to say, he was in seventh heaven with his playwright in tow. I can't understand people like Dickie: what fun do they get out of always being second fiddle? After the Caprice I went over to Steven's new apartment on the river; it's in a remodelled tenement house and I must say it's fun, and the Queen Anne desk I sold him looks perfect heaven in his living-room. I'll say one thing for him: Steven is one of the few

people who has the good sense simply to let a fine piece
go in a room. There were quite a few people there and
we had New York champagne which is drinkable when
you're already full of vodka. Needless to say, Steven
pulled me off to one corner to ask about Bob. I wish
people wouldn't be so sympathetic, not that they really
are of course, but they feel they must *pretend* to be:
actually they're only curious. I said Bob *seemed* all right
when I saw him last month. I didn't go into any details
though Steven did his best to worm the whole story out
of me. Fortunately, I have a good grip on myself nowadays and I am able to talk about the break-up quite
calmly. I always tell everybody I hope Bob will do well
in his new business and that I like Sydney very much.
Actually, I hear things are going badly, that the shop is
doing *no* business and that Bob is drinking again which
means he's busy cruising the streets and getting into
trouble. Well, I'm out of it and any day now I'll meet
somebody – though it's funny how seldom you see
anyone who's really attractive. There was a nice young
Swede at Steven's, but I never did get his name and
anyway he is being kept by that ribbon clerk from the
Madison Avenue Store. After Steven's I went to a real
brawl in the Village: a studio apartment, packed with
people, dozens of new faces, too. I wish now I hadn't got
so drunk because there were some really attractive
people there. I was all set, I thought, to go home with
one but the friend intervened at the last moment and it
looked for a moment like there was going to be real
trouble before our host separated us. I never did get the
host's name, I think he's in advertising. So I ended up
alone. Must call doctor about hepatitis pills, write Leonore Fini, check last month's invoices (re missing Shera-
ton receipt), call Mrs. Blaine-Smith about sofa.

27th December, 1953

I finally had tea with Mrs. Blaine-Smith today, one of the most beautiful women I've ever met, so truly chic and well-dressed. I'm hopelessly indebted to Steven for bringing us together: she practically keeps the shop going. She had only six or seven people for tea, very much *en famille*, and I couldn't've been more surprised and pleased when she asked me to stay on. (I expect she knows what a discount I gave her on that Hepplewhite sofa.) Anyway, one of her guests was an Italian count who was terribly nice though unattractive. We sat next to each other on that delicious ottoman in the library and chatted about Europe after the war: what a time that was! I told him I hadn't been back since 1948 but even so we knew quite a few people in common. Then, as always, the name Elliott Magren was mentioned. He's practically a codeword – if you know Elliott, well, you're on the inside – and of course the Count (as I'd expected all along) knew Elliott and we exchanged bits of information about him, skirting carefully drugs and small boys because Mrs. Blaine-Smith though she knows everyone (and everything) *never* alludes to that sort of thing in any way; such a relief after so many of the queen bees you run into. Hilda, for instance, who married the maddest designer in Los Angeles and gives, I am told, the crudest parties with everyone drunk from morning till night. (Must stop drinking so much: nothing *after* dinner, that's the secret, especially with my liver. We were discussing Elliott's apartment in the Rue du Bac and that marvellous Tchelichew that hangs over his bed when a little Englishman, whose name I never did get, turned and said: 'Did you know that Elliott Magren died last week?' I must say it was stunning news, sitting in Mrs. Blaine-Smith's library so far, far away. . . . The Count was even more upset than I (could he have been one of Elliott's numerous admirers?) I couldn't help recalling then that terrible time at Deauville when Elliott was arrested and I had had to put up bail for him and hire a lawyer, all in French! Suddenly everything came back to me in a flood: that summer, the affair with Hilda, and Helen (incidentally, just this morning got a Christmas card from Helen, the first word in years: a photograph of her husband and three ghastly children, all living in Toledo: well, I suppose she's happy). But what an important summer that was: the chrysalis burst at last which, I think, prepared me for all the bad luck later when I failed my doctorate and had to go to work in Steven's office. . . . And now Elliott's dead. Hard to believe someone you once knew is actually dead, not like the war where sudden absences in the roster were taken for granted. The Englishman told us the whole story. It seems Elliott was rounded up in a police raid on dope addicts in which a number of very famous people were caught, too. He was told to leave the country; so he piled everything into two taxicabs and drove to the Gare St. Lazare where he took a train for Rome. He settled down in a small apartment off the Via Veneto. Last autumn he underwent another series of shock treatment, administered by a quack doctor who cured him of drugs but lost his memory for him in the process. Apart from this, he was in good health and looked as young as ever except that for some reason he dyed his hair red – too mad! Then, last week, he made a date to go to the opera with a friend. The friend arrived, the door was open but, inside, there was no Elliott. The friend was particularly annoyed because Elliott often would not show up at all if, en route to an appointment, he happened to see someone desirable in the street. I remember Elliott telling me once that his greatest pleasure was to follow a handsome stranger for hours on end through the streets of a city. It was not so much the chase which interested him as the identification he had with the boy he followed: he would become the other, imitating his gestures, his gait, becoming himself young, absorbed in a boy's life. But Elliott had followed no one that day. The friend finally found him face down in the bathroom, dead. When the autopsy was performed, it was discovered that Elliott had had a malformed heart, an extremely rare case, and he might have died as suddenly at any moment in his life. The drugs, the shock treatment and so on had contributed nothing to his death. He was buried Christmas day in the Protestant cemetery close to Shelley, in good company to the end. I must say I can't imagine him with red hair. The Count asked me to have dinner with him tomorrow at the Colony (!) and I said I'd be delighted. Then Mrs. Blaine-Smith told the most devastating story about the Duchess of Windsor in Palm Beach.

Find out about Helen Gleason's sphinxes. Call Bob about the keys to the back closet. Return Steven's copy of *Valmouth*. Find out the Count's name before dinner tomorrow.

1956

The Ladies in the Library

for *Alice Bouverie*

I

He seldom saw his cousin Sybil, and he was always ill-at-ease on those occasions when they did meet, for she still represented the Family: a vague and now spent force which had been in a process of dissolution ever since his college days some twenty years earlier, diminishing not only as a force but as a fact until today only the two of them were left.

She lived in Baltimore and he lived in New York. Neither had married, a clear indication that nature had abandoned yet another experiment in eugenics. In other times he had occasionally tried to imagine himself as a father with numerous children in whose healthy veins his essence would be precipitated into future time, ensuring for him that posterity of blood which so appeals to those who briefly see eternity in man, but unfortunately neither the literal nor the metaphysical image ever concretized properly in his imagination, much less in life; and now, middle-aged, he assumed the conditions of his bachelor existence were fixed, the danger of serious change remote.

Sybil too had neglected to marry; and although she still made cosy allusions to weddings and Christmas parties, to Easter egg hunts and funerals, to all the beloved activities of a family's life, in actual fact, she had consigned most human relationships to pleasant memory, devoting her life instead to dogs and cats, her dealings with these dependent creatures not unlike those she might have enjoyed with the children she never bore, with the family that had died. In a sense of course all things were nearly equal: she gave Christmas parties for the dogs and she made matches for the cats, arranging their destinies with the energy of a matriarch and, certainly, with better luck than matriarchs usually enjoy in the world of people.

'We have nothing in common,' he thought, as he waited for her in the Union station, the dome of the Capitol like an elaborate dessert framed in the doorway. 'We would never have known one another if we had not been first cousins, but then, to be precise, we do not *know* each other now.' With a wetted forefinger he tried to paste back one corner of a curling Excelsior Hotel sticker which threatened to tear off the way the Continental, Paris, and the El Minzah, Tangier had, leaving his suitcase messy with shreds of bright-coloured paper making no design at all, none at all.

'Ah, there you are, Walter. I'm sorry if I'm late. But then I don't think I *am* late. Here, let my porter take your bag; he's a gem.' The gem took his suitcase, and as they walked to the train, she asked him about New York. But he had no intention of telling her anything about New York while she, he knew, had every intention of discussing Baltimore, the dogs and the cats, and then, more soon than late, she would talk about the Family, about that race of Virginia cavaliers, the Bragnets, who, except for the two of them, had seen fit to vanish in the first half of the twentieth century, leaving no monument except the house they had built near Winchester so many, many years ago when the country was new and rich and their apple orchards were still

saplings, without blossoms or fruit or history. The name
of Bragnet on her lips was always strange and marvellous, as though she were intoning, priestess-like, the secret
name of a deity, a name which could blast trees, shatter
stone, separate lovers, cause twins to be born joined,
curdle cream and, best of all, re-create the house of their
common memory with the graceful, long-dead figures of
those Bragnets who now lay in the dust of the Episcopal
cemetery at Winchester.

But she was not herself today, for even after they had
taken their seats in the train and he had arranged their
suitcases on the rack overhead she did not pronounce
the magic name. She wanted deliberately to mystify
him, he decided irritably, and the only way he could
retaliate was to ask no questions, to pretend it made no
difference to him that for the first time in twenty years
he was returning to Winchester, at her inscrutable request.

'I've had such a busy time in Washington this week,'
said Sybil. 'We had several really creative meetings of
the Dog Society . . . oh, I know what you feel about our
work. I've given up trying to convert you.' She laughed
heartily; she was blonde-grey, untidy, and as old, he
recalled, as their splendid century, but unlike the century not scarred at all. Sybil belonged to quite another
time, to a world of serene country life where dogs mat-
tered and horses were ridden, where men and women
remained married, despite all differences: a legendary
age where emotion had been contained shrewdly by a
formal manner which, in its turn, could only flourish in
great houses, in high-ceilinged rooms with massive
doors and bright brass. Sybil belonged to that world in
spirit if not in fact, and although she lived in a very
small house in Baltimore her whole being suggested vast

lawns and ordered gardens: boxwood, clipped and severe, muting the brilliance of roses: formal gardens set in wild uncharted country.

'I never knew that you knew Miss Mortimer,' he said at last, forestalling a full report on the health and adventures of her animal friends in Baltimore.

'Oh, I've known her for years. As a matter of fact, I was in the house the day your mother decided to sell the place to her, and I've always made it a point to keep in touch, because of the house.'

Walter, at this point, was inclined to reminisce about the house (most conversations, it often seemed to him, were no more than competing monologues: a condition which he accepted as human and natural, a part of the universal strangeness), but Sybil had resolutely embarked upon Miss Mortimer. 'A sweet, sweet woman. You'll adore her, although people don't always, at least not at first. I'm not sure why. Perhaps because she *seems* sad, and of course you never really know *what* she'll say or do. Not that I mean she's eccentric: she's not one of those women who'll do anything for an effect. No, she's quite serious and she has her own little set in Winchester. The Parker family are especially close to her. You remember the girls, don't you? The three sisters? They're all married now and all three live in Winchester. Isn't that remarkable, keeping so close together? No, I'm really devoted to her. And I've told her so much about you. Why, she's even read one of your books. Anyway, we both decided that after all these years it was time you two got together.'

'Now it was out,' he thought glumly. Sybil was trying to make a match, doubtless to get Bragnet House back into the family again. It was childishly clear: if he married Miss Mortimer and went to live at Bragnet, Sybil would once again have a marvellous big place to keep her dogs and cats. He looked at her suspiciously, but she had again shifted the subject: she asked him about his life in New York, inquired graciously if he had written anything new.

'I'm always working.' He hated to be asked what he was doing because the temptation to answer at length was so great. Briefly, he told her his plans for the season. And then, upon request, he named their mutual friends one by one, and if she liked them he very subtly made them out worse than they were, while if she disliked them he discovered heretofore unsuspected virtues in their characters. Neither took the ritual of this conversation very seriously; they were not half done when, like the sudden tolling of a bell, Sybil at last pronounced the name of Bragnet.

'We are the last,' she said, with a rich melancholy pride, 'you and I. Strange how a family dies out. There were so many Bragnets fifty years ago and now there are only two . . . and the house.'

'Which is no longer ours.'

'Your mother should never have sold it, never.'

'It was too big for us,' said Walter, and then, before Sybil could embark on that line, he asked if there were to be other guests for the week-end.

'Only her nephew. He's supposed to be very bright. He's still in school. I suppose he'll inherit the house.' She paused, and Walter noticed she was uneasy, unlike her usual self. 'Oh, you'll like her,' she added disjointedly. 'I just know you will.'

'Why *shouldn't* I?'

'Well, one's friends don't always like each other, do they? And she *is* a little difficult to know . . . rather unnerving at first: but that's only because she's shy.'

'I promise not to be terrified.'

'I'm sure you won't be.' On that odd note the conversation lapsed and both for a long time studied the green countryside beyond the telephone-poles which sped past with regularity of pentameter in a blank verse tragedy.

II

As far as the eye could see to the south the apple trees grew in ordered ranks upon the rolling land, their leaves glittering green and new and their fruit green too, not yet ripe. Among the orchards, on a hill a mile removed from the asphalt highway, stood the lawn-circled house where Walter Bragnet was born and where his family had lived for so many generations in one long golden season of comfort, untouched by the wars, made rich by their orchards and sustained from century to century by a proud serenity which was, his cousin Sybil maintained, inspired by the earth in these parts as well as by the rose-red brick house with its Greek Revival colonnade, the last tangible expression of the Bragnet family now reduced to two travellers who, with week-end valises, were deposited by a taxi-cab before the front door of their old home.

As he rang the door-bell, he wondered what he should feel or, more important, what he *did* feel, but as usual he could not determine. He would have to wait until he could safely recall this scene in memory; only in the future could he ever discover what, if anything, he had felt; he existed almost entirely in recollection, a peculiarity of considerable value to him as a writer, though disastrous in his life since no event could touch him until it was safely past, until alone in bed at night he could experience in a rush all the emotions he had been unable to feel at the appropriate time; then he would writhe, knowing it was again too late to act.

The door opened and they were admitted by a Negro in a white jacket, an acquaintance of Sybil's. They inquired solicitously of one another, as Walter followed them up the familiar staircase. The rooms were burdened with the same odour of musty linen, of roses and of wood smoke which he remembered from his childhood. On the walls of the upstairs corridor hung the same Gillray prints which his grandfather had brought back from England; and, finally, the room to which he was shown was the one he had lived in for nearly eighteen years. He glanced sharply at Sybil, suspecting her of stage-managing: but she only looked at him blandly and remarked: 'This used to be your room, didn't it?'

He nodded and followed the servant into his old room: a four-poster bed of pale scarred wood with no canopy, a fire-place with brass phoenixes to support the logs and, amazingly enough, his books were still on the shelves of the bookcase where he had left them the day he went off to college. He had always presumed that when his mother sold the house she'd given them away: obviously she had not, and here they were: the Oz books, the Arabian Nights, Greek mythology. . . .

Sybil went, and he dressed for dinner; then he walked about the room, touching the books, but not taking them down, repelling with a certain pleasure whatever force it was that insisted he look at them, become even more involved in Sybil's obscure plot. 'If she thinks that I'll try to get the house back she's mistaken,' he murmured to his own image in the mirror above the chest of drawers. He noticed that his face was flushed as though he had been drinking. It was the heat, he decided, as Sybil rapped on his door and then, before he could speak, proceeded briskly into the room, plain and unfashionable in gossamer grey and wearing yellow diamonds. 'I thought we would go down together since you don't know her.'

'Together by all means,' he said genially, and together they went down the staircase, moving decorously, tactful among ghosts.

In the drawing-room, Miss Mortimer came forward to meet them, and Walter experienced an inexplicable panic; fortunately, Sybil began to talk. 'Well, here he is!' she said, embracing her hostess. 'I promised I'd bring him, and I did!'

'And now he's here,' said Miss Mortimer with a smile; her voice was low and he found that he had to be most attentive if he wanted to hear what she said, and he did want to hear, very much. She took his hand in her cool one and drew him over to a sofa. 'You have no idea how happy I am to see you at last. Sybil has talked so much about you. I've asked her many times to bring you here, but you never came.' They sat down, side by side.

'I've been very busy,' said Walter, blushing. He paused and then repeated: 'I've been very busy.' He looked to Sybil, mysteriously helpless; she gave him bright succour, from her wealth of small talk, she tossed a penny to Miss Mortimer: 'Where is that nephew of yours? Where's Stephen?' And Miss Mortimer told them that her nephew would be along presently, that he had been riding all day: he had only just got home. 'I am afraid at times I hardly understand him,' she smiled at Walter.

'Is he so difficult?' Walter was becoming more used to her, to the situation. She was handsome with regular features, dark hair and eyes, only her mouth was bad, thin and forbidding. She was tall and she sat very straight beside him, her white hands folded in her lap.

'No, not difficult, just strange to me. Others are charmed by him. I expect he's going through a phase, and of course when he's older I'll have more in common with him. At the moment he's almost too energetic. He rides horses; he writes poems.'

Walter wondered if he would be asked to read the boy's poems, to advise him whether or not to pursue a career of letters. He began to rehearse in his mind his set speech on the vicissitudes of the literary life.

'Yes, Mr. Bragnet, he is at *that* stage. He even has a lady friend, a Winchester girl whom he sees every evening.'

Walter looked at her with interest, wondering why she should want to discuss her nephew in such detail. There was something quite un-Virginian in her lack of reticence, and he liked her a little more for this.

The nephew entered the room so quietly that Walter was not aware of him until he saw by Miss Mortimer's expression that there was someone behind him. He turned and then, as the boy approached, he rose and they shook hands. Miss Mortimer performed the introductions; then Stephen sat down in a chair between Sybil and Walter, closing the half-circle before the empty fire-place. Sybil asked him numerous questions while Walter listened to neither the questions nor the answers. The boy was uncommonly good-looking, with blond hair and skin dark from the sun, the face not yet coarsened by the grain of a beard. Walter was reminded of himself at the same age, living in this house, coming home at vacation time. . . . He glanced suddenly at Miss Mortimer, who had been watching him; she nodded gravely, as though she had divined his mood and wanted now to console him with truth rather than with pity: *she* knew how fine it was to be young, in this house. He wondered if he liked her any better for having understood.

Stephen was speaking: 'I rode over to the Parker place this afternoon. . . .'

'Did Emily ride with you?' asked Miss Mortimer. Walter knew that Emily must be the summer beloved, traditional figure of green and yellow light.

'No, she didn't,' said the boy curtly, looking at his aunt with bright cold eyes. 'I went alone, and I saw old Mrs. Parker, who told me to tell you the girls will be over for lunch tomorrow.'

'I'm so glad!' said Sybil. 'I haven't seen them in years. You remember them, Walter?'

'Certainly.' He recalled three sisters: Claudia, Alice and . . . Laura? But they would hardly be girls now, he thought. They would be middle-aged strangers, inquisitive, tiresome. Restlessly, he shifted his position, faced Stephen more squarely, his back to Miss Mortimer. While Sybil recalled with wonder and pleasure how the girls had all managed to marry Winchester men, Stephen sat straight and polite, his brown fingers interlaced, his eyes on his aunt. Walter wondered why they disliked one another so openly. It was obvious to him that there could be little sympathy between two such dissimilar people; yet this open warfare seemed inappropriate, considering the essential casualness of their relationship.

'I hope you'll show Mr. Bragnet some of your poems, Stephen. He's a writer, you know.'

'Yes, I know,' said Stephen, smiling, and Walter froze, aware that he was no longer admired, that his vogue had ended many years ago, and that other writers now claimed the attention of the young and earnest.

'I should like to see them,' said Walter, almost sincerely, enchanted with the boy's apparent ease, with his vitality; and he admired Stephen even more when, with an implacable grace, he faced Miss Mortimer and said: 'I never show them to anyone.' Then he turned quickly to Walter. 'I mean I don't like to have people read them because they aren't very good and because they're private. You know what I mean, don't you?'

'Indeed I do,' began Walter.

'By the way,' interrupted Miss Mortimer, 'why don't you ask Emily to come over for lunch tomorrow? You know I want to meet her. It would be great fun.'

'Yes, it would,' said Stephen ironically, cutting short this flanking movement. 'I'm sure she'd like to ... but she can't tomorrow. She wants so much to meet *you*,' he added, grinning.

'Well, another time.' And Miss Mortimer serenely accepted checkmate.

'My gracious Stephen, aren't you awfully young to be having a lady friend?' asked Sybil with that clumsy teasing tone which she often used with the larger dogs. Walter wondered if there were some way in which he might align himself with Stephen against the two women. But his assistance was not needed. Stephen laughed and said: 'No, I don't think I am.' Then Miss Mortimer led them all into the dining-room where paintings of colonial Bragnets still hung upon the walls, rich by candle-light.

'We *must* get the family portraits away from you,' said Sybil.

III

The next day luncheon was dinner, and though much too elaborate, too heavy for a hot day, Walter ate greedily. He had spent a restless night in the bed of his childhood and now he was tired, exhausted from lack of sleep. The Parker sisters were a further nuisance. They irritated him unreasonably. Now middle-aged, they were resolutely jolly and appallingly confident. After lunch, still gabbling, the sisters sat side by side on a sofa in the library. 'Like judges,' thought Walter, loosening his belt, feeling ill. He was wondering if he should go to his room for pills (he took many pills; his heart murmured) when Miss Mortimer turned to him and they talked intimately and at length of dreams, of a particular dream he had had the night before (he had found himself in a black sea, drowning).

Miss Mortimer appeared youthful today, even desirable, and he wondered how he could have had such a disagreeable first impression of her. During lunch she had talked to him of his books, and long before the over-rich pudding had been served, he realized that she was not only intelligent but uncannily sensitive to mood, knowing when to praise, when to chide. He had not felt so easy with a new person in many years. She even divined his physical discomfort, for, suddenly, she suggested he go to Stephen outside on the terrace where she would join them presently. Both excused themselves, and the Parker sisters, busy now with their knitting and their judgments, seemed not in the least annoyed, so perfectly at home were they, so used to one another's company. Even Sybil defected to observe the old stables.

The sun was hot, its light undiffused by clouds; for a moment Walter stood on the terrace, dizzy and blind. Then Stephen spoke to him. 'You escaped.'

'Yes.' The world righted itself and Walter saw the green lawn before him, bending towards orchards. 'I escaped.'

Stephen pulled two deck-chairs together and they sat down. Walter was alarmed to find that he felt no better; could the sun be bad for him? His heart thumped irregularly. His pulses fluttered.

'You lived in this house, didn't you?'

Walter nodded. 'I was about your age when I went away to college. While I was gone, my mother sold the place and we moved to Washington.'

'Did you like living here?'

'Oh, very much: don't you?'

'I like the place itself,' said the boy slowly. 'I like to ride. . . .'

'But you don't like your aunt.' He was suddenly too tired and too ill to keep to the periphery; it was easier to go to the centre immediately.

'No, I don't like her, I never have.' He smiled. 'She says I'll understand her better when I'm older.'

'Perhaps you will.' Both were silent then. Neither chose to pursue this indiscreet, unchivalrous duologue.

Stephen played idly with a large winged ant and Walter watched as the ant would climb the boy's thumb, only to be pulled back, to begin again its laborious ascent. Little beads of perspiration gleamed on Stephen's brown forehead and his hair glittered in the sun. Finally, the ant escaped. 'I'm going to take a walk. You want to come with me?'

'No, I had better stay here.' Walter wanted to go, but he did not dare; with a sudden, inexplicable sorrow, he watched the boy walk across the lawn. Not till he was out of sight did Walter shut his eyes and rest. Murmuring summer held him. Sharp, sweet odour of new-cut grass; croaking of frogs in a distant pond. He was nearly asleep when he heard voices: the ladies in the library were discussing him. He knew that he should get up and walk away, but he did not stir.

'He never married. I wonder why.' Walter could identify none of the voices: the sisters spoke alike.

'Not the sort.'

'I hate it when they have no children. Oh, I know it's sentimental. . . .'

'Well, he has none, and that's that, and we have our work to do. He's had a pleasant time.'

'I should say so, and he missed all our wars. How did he manage that?'

'Heart condition.'

'I suspect that *that's* our cue.'

'Does he still write?'

'No, he seems to have given up.'

'At fifty-one: that's rather early. Perhaps if he were to have another few years, an even sixty . . .'

'No! It *must* be now!'

They lowered their voices then and talked of knitting – one of them had found a knot in her yarn; they also talked of accidents and diseases, and he listened less attentively, shaken by what he had heard, wondering if he might not still be dreaming: how could these women have known so much about his life, so many things not even his closest friends knew?

'. . . run down by a cab in front of the Union Station.'

'Oh, not that, not *that*!'

'Blood poisoning? A scratch? A fever . . .?'

'Out of character. There *is* time, you know: no reason to clutch at straws.'

'The heart, I suppose . . . *again*.'

'And why not? Why confect some elaborate plot when procedure is so clearly indicated? There's no reason to be bizarre.'

'Very well: the heart . . . But when? Miss Mortimer is restless.'

'Tomorrow on the train, as he lifts his suitcase to put it on the rack . . .?'

'No, not another day. I mean, look . . . it's already strung out to the end. Besides, Miss Mortimer's already out there on the terrace, waiting for us, poor angel.'

'I'm afraid I can't get this last knot undone.'

'Then use scissors. Here.'

He could neither speak nor move now. He was conscious of a massive constriction in his chest. As he gasped for breath, nearly blind in the sun, Miss Mortimer appeared to him over the edge of the receding world, and he saw that she was smiling, a summer flower in her gleaming hair, a familiar darkness in her lovely eyes.

1950

THE   END